The Strange Curse of Breda

By Steven Arnett

This book is entirely a work of fiction. The names, characters, and incidents portrayed in it are the work of the author's imagination. Any resemblance to actual persons, living or dead, events or places, are entirely coincidental. It is not in any way meant to disparage the Dutch people who settle in West Michigan in the 1800s and have been an enormous American success story.

Dedicated to my godson Gerad Carrillo

Chapter 1

February 9, 1889

It was a perfect morning for a hanging. Streaks of light pink and orange silhouetted the snow, sand hills, and pines as Sheriff Jacob Feikema, his deputy Christen Postma, the Reverend Pieter Van Riper, and the condemned man, Obadiah Kurtz, rode to the makeshift gallows that had been built the day before about a mile outside of town. None of the men spoke, and the silence was broken only by the crunch of wagon wheels in the snow. It was the coldest morning that Reverend Van Riper could remember, and he wondered whether it was just the temperature or partly the grimness of their task that made the cold seem to cut to the bone. He decided it was more than the weather. He felt as if there was a cold wind blowing through his soul. He knew that Kurtz wasn't guilty, that he'd been railroaded to the gallows by a town that didn't understand him, that was afraid of him, and had jumped at the chance to rid themselves of him after his wife Jessie had died mysteriously.

The men were from Breda, which was founded in 1851 by Reverend Van Riper's father-in-law, the Reverend Heinrik Wijhe, and his followers. Wijhe had left the original Dutch settlement in west Michigan after a falling out with its leader, Dr. Albertus C. Van Raalte. The falling out had to do with ideology—a disagreement about free will and atonement for sin—that led to a bitter break between the two men. Reverend Wijhe's dark and apocalyptic vision led him to believe that even the staunchly devout Dr. Van Raalte would not escape perdition.

The men remained silent as they stopped at the gallows, and Obadiah was led down from the wagon by Deputy Postma. Feikema and Postma and Van Riper were all relieved there'd been no outburst from the prisoner, no more of the ranting speeches about his innocence and the curses that were going to fall upon them. They'd heard those speeches from Obadiah more times than they could count. They were seared into their minds and their consciences. Reverend Van Riper opened his Bible to Psalm 17 and read:

Arise, O Lord, disappoint him, cast him down: Deliver my soul from the wicked, which is thy sword: From men which are thy hand, from men of the world, Which have this portion in this life,

And whose belly thou fillest with thy hid treasure: They are full of children and leave their substance to their babes.

As he read, he was afraid to look up into the condemned man's eyes, even though Obadiah was staring right at him. Every sound seemed magnified. Reverend Van Riper thought he could feel Obadiah's eyes pierce through him amid the swish of the wind and the melancholy song of a bird singing deep in the woods. Then the outburst began that cut through the good reverend like a sword of ice.

"Here today is committed a great travesty against justice," Obadiah shouted. "For you who carry it out, I proclaim a curse on you and your children through all the generations. And to your town. Someday my sons or the sons of my sons shall come back and bring a plague to Breda. Your wives and your children and their children shall suffer death at the hands of Satan, shall curse the day they were born."

Reverend Van Riper and Sheriff Feikema and Deputy Postma stood frozen as solidly into the ground as the pines and maples that surrounded them.

"Your wives and daughters shall become whores and your children will beg before Satan. A deathly pestilence shall sweep over the town."

Finally, Feikema grabbed Obadiah—who's feet were tied and who's hands were tied behind his back—and shook him.

"Stop it!" he shouted. "Shut your damn mouth!" and he slapped him across the face with all his strength. But Obadiah didn't even seem to feel it.

"What are you going to do about it, kill me?" Obadiah taunted, with the most terrifying smile that any of them had ever seen. For some time, none of the others spoke. They were mute with horror and loathing and guilt.

"There'll be no more prayers," Feikema finally said. "The time has come to carry out the judgment of the court."

He and Postma took hold of Obadiah and began to lead him toward the gallows. But Obadiah tried to get away from them, and it took all their strength to keep him from breaking away.

"Locusts shall come from out of the bowels of the earth and eat up your harvests. You shall starve in the infamy of endless winter!" Obadiah went on.

He kept talking and struggled with all his strength as Feikema and Postma dragged him to the gallows as the sun rose in a red ball over Lake Michigan. Feikema and Postma sweated beneath their heavy woolen coats with the intensity of their labor, despite the piercing wind that was blowing off the frozen lake. Reverend Van Riper looked away.

Finally, somehow, they got Obadiah to the top of the gallows and put the noose snuggly around his neck.

"This is your last chance to avoid eternal damnation," Obadiah shouted. "No forgiveness can ever occur!"

But Feikema knew there could be no going back now. His hand shaking almost beyond control, he pulled the lever and heard the heavy thud as Obadiah dropped through the floor of the gallows and dangled in the cold wind. Feikema wanted to look away, and so did the others, but somehow their eyes were inexorably drawn to Obadiah's grotesque, twisted face and body as he swung gently back and forth. And then there was just the swish of the snow again, and the lone bird still singing plaintively, and the creaking of the wood of the gallows. Then there weren't even those sounds, just an empty silence that seemed to the three men like a death sentence over the whole world.

Chapter 2

September 15, 1971

Jane Lucas knew she was too wasted to be driving, but the party she'd been at had turned into a bad scene, and she had to leave. A guy had been hitting on her all night, and he'd gotten more aggressive the later it got. The other people were starting to get on her nerves, too. She was drunk, and she'd smoked some killer weed and done some speed, and the effect of the three together toward the end was that the room seemed to whirl around, the faces all seemed to turn toward her and smile in a bizarre, evil, accusing way. She'd felt paranoia that verged on panic.

As she drove, the road seemed to move. It seemed like a black, menacing strip with a life of its own, and she had to concentrate hard to stay in the lane. Fortunately, she thought, I'm way out in the sticks, and I'm not likely to run into any cops. She was only 19, but her life was a pretty big mess. She'd dropped out of school when she was sixteen and been heavy into the drug scene, and the two rehab centers her parents had put her in had only kept her clean for a few months. She'd also had two abortions and hadn't worked anywhere for more than a few months at a time. Her last job was working at the counter at Burger

King, but she'd been fired for missing work and coming in late. Lately, though, she'd been thinking about turning her life around, of getting off drugs and going back to school and eventually going to college. There was a guy she really had it bad for, Jason Macklin, and she knew she'd never get anywhere with him the way she was now. He wasn't the only reason she wanted to change. He wasn't even the main reason. But she thought if she and Jason were together, she could change her whole life, get a brand new start.

Lighting another Salem, she thought that by the time she finished it, she'd be back at her apartment. But then she saw someone up ahead, right in the middle of the road. He was flagging her down. If she hadn't known who it was, she never would have stopped—it's too dangerous with all the kooks there are in the world today, she thought, and I'm out in the middle of nowhere—but she recognized him. She didn't exactly know the guy, didn't even know his name. He was new to town as far as she knew, but she'd seen him in Breda lately. She didn't want to stop. She thought, what a hassle this is, but she was sure he could see who she was, and she didn't want to be embarrassed if she happened to run into him again in town. Pulling off onto the shoulder of the road, she wearily rolled down the window.

"I was wondering if you could give me a ride into town," the guy said. "My car broke down on me."

"Sure," she said. "Get in."

She slurred the words, and he seemed to sneer at her like the people at the party. He got in the car beside her, but just as she was about to pull back on the road, he reached over and turned the car off and pulled the keys out.

"Actually, I'm in no hurry to get back to town," he said, smiling, grabbing her by the arm and holding her so tight it felt like his fingers were going to break through her skin. "We've got something to take care of, you and me."

He opened the door and dragged her outside as she screamed like she was being dragged into hell, even though she knew, perhaps, that screaming was useless. No house was within half a mile. He dragged her into the woods far enough so that no one passing by on the road could have seen them. She tried to get away with all her might, but she was weak from the drugs and booze in her system, and he seemed incredibly strong to her for his size. But she *was* finally able to get away after she bit his arm hard, and she ran toward the road.

He ran after her and caught her, but they were close enough now to the road that anyone driving by could easily see them. He panicked. Pain was surging through his body from her bite. He knew he should try to drag her further back into the woods but was afraid if he did, she might escape again, and his arm was weakened from the bite. He wasn't sure he would have the strength or courage to catch her if she did get away again. So he threw her onto the ground and sat on her right there. He tried to stab her as she scratched and punched him, at the same time terrified that a car would come down the road. Her screaming rattled him, horrified him. Murdering Jane Lucas was much more difficult than he'd imagined it would be, and he'd imagined it a thousand times. She was putting up much more of a struggle than he'd ever imagined she could. Finally, though, his knife hit home. He stabbed her repeatedly, almost aimlessly at first, but eventually he got her in the throat. The blood gurgled as it poured out and in no time at all, she stopped struggling and lay there lifeless.

"I don't like it," Jack Booth said. "I don't like it one bit."

He was talking about the commune that had recently been set up on a farm not far from town. Jim Leiden nodded his head, not in agreement but because he preferred not to say anything about it. He didn't want to say anything that would start Booth off on a tirade.

"I don't know why they came here," Booth went on. "They must not have realized what kind of community this is. And Bill Mathers acts like there's not a damn thing he can do about it," speaking of the county sheriff. "Well, some of us just may take the matter into our own hands if he doesn't."

Jack Booth was probably the most conservative man in Breda, Michigan. He was a member of the John Birch society and a faithful reader of the *National Review*. Some said he'd once been in the Ku Klux Klan.

"I don't suppose there's much he can do if they haven't broken any laws," Jim said, feeling at this point that he had to say something. "I Am the Walrus" by the Beatles was playing softly on the radio by the cash register.

"Laws, my ass," his voice and temper rising. "Do you really think they don't have a stash of drugs out there, pot and LSD and who knows what else? They look like the Manson family. Who knows what they might do?"

Jim began putting cans of Campbell's pork and beans on the shelf of his small store. He hated Jack Booth. Not because of his politics—he was almost completely apolitical himself—he just didn't like the man, and he didn't like the way he'd come into the store and just hang around bitching about everything. But he did a lot of business at the store, so what else could he do but tolerate him? Booth especially annoyed him today because Jim was in an unusually thoughtful mood. He was wondering if he and his fiancée, Julie Veere, would ever get married. He'd thought about it before, but he never got tired of thinking about it. She was the only thing that made his life worthwhile.

The store really belonged to his father and mother, but his father—who mostly lived off a disability pension from World War II—was drunk too much of the time to run it, and his mother was too scatterbrained and irresponsible. Jim didn't really like running the store, and when he was growing up, he swore to himself he'd never end up there. A million other things there were he would rather have done and a million other places he'd rather have lived. The town held a lot of bad memories for him, and he would just as soon have left it forever. But the place meant a lot to his mother. It had been in her family for a hundred years, and Jim felt that out of love and loyalty to her, he had to take care of it. There was no one else to do it. His older sister, Cheryl, wouldn't have done it for a million dollars a year. She was a fashion buyer in Chicago and could hardly stand to spend a weekend in Breda, much less live there and manage the store. Also, Jim didn't think she'd ever felt loyalty to anything. She was already on her third husband, for Christ's sake. Tall and sandy haired, Jim still had the muscles of the star high school athlete that he had been not many years before. He had an all-American look, but there was a mature, thoughtful look in his blue eyes that made him seem older than he really was. It was a look that also made many young women fall for him.

Even the love and loyalty Jim felt for his mother probably wouldn't have kept him in Breda indefinitely, though, if it hadn't been for Julie. He'd known her since they were about three, but he hadn't seen her much since high school until she'd come into the store on a rainy day. No one else was there. They got to talking, first about what had happened to people they'd known in school. Then it had started raining so hard that it would have been crazy for her to leave, and they'd gone in the back of the store and sat down and talked for hours. Jim could never remember laughing so hard or being so funny himself, and he'd never forget the sound of the rain on the roof, and the taste of the cheese and crackers they'd eaten. Before she left, he and Julie had a date, and he was sure he was in love with her.

Jim became so lost in thought, he didn't notice when Jack Booth walked out. Jim wondered if he'd offended him by not listening to him intently enough and shrugged as if to say, if I did, so be it. There was nothing he could do about it now. He went on restocking the shelves, and when Julie walked in, he wondered if somehow she knew he'd been thinking about her. She had almost black hair that made a lovely contrast to her soft, fair skin and blue eyes that shined with intelligence and beauty—eyes that showed, if not innocence, at least a freshness and openness to the world that hadn't been corrupted yet by cynicism. She was slender, and her figure was beautifully shaped.

"Jim, the most awful thing has happened," she said. "Jane Lucas has been murdered, and apparently it was some kind of cult thing. She was stabbed, and some weird symbols were written on her body."

Jim recalled what Jack Booth had said and a chill went through him. Julie came over and hugged him, and he felt her gently shaking. He had a sick feeling and didn't say anything for a while because he had no idea what to say. Nothing like that had ever happened in Breda.

"Does anyone know who did it?" he finally said.

"Oh, no. The body was just found about an hour ago."

"I really feel bad for her folks. They've gone through so much with her."

Jim paused, paused because he still didn't really have the slightest idea of what the appropriate words were for the situation.

"The Lucas's are such a nice couple," he finally went on. "My heart really goes out to them."

Just then Jerry Wilkens burst into the store. "Did you hear what happened?" he said.

"Yeah, Julie just told me," Jim said. "What do you know about it?"

"Just that Al Purtan found her body on his farm in the woods off Crackling Road. She was cut up with a knife, and there were some letters written in blood on her body.

Half the cops in west Michigan are out there right now. I hear they're even going to bring the FBI in."

Harriet Erskine and her husband, Elmer, the two most notorious gossips in town, came into the store next, and then George Hepfinger and Billy Wine. Before long, the store was filled with people talking about the murder, and no one was buying anything, and everybody was saying the same things over and over in slightly different words. Everyone seemed to derive some comfort and a feeling of safety from being with the others and talking about what had happened, even though most of them were scared as hell. Jim got tired pretty fast of hearing everyone talk. He finally ended up going outside with Julie, so he could get away from them and talk to her alone.

"I'm worried about you," Jim said. "You're so vulnerable out there in the country with just your mom."

"Don't be silly, Jim. There isn't any reason to believe anyone else will be murdered. We have no idea what was behind it. Considering the crowd she hung out with, sad to say, there's probably some kind of drug connection. There isn't any reason for you to worry about me."

But that didn't make Jim feel much better. As Julie drove away, he had a sickening feeling. There was no way he was going to be able to keep from worrying about Julie until he knew why Jane Lucas had been killed.

Driving home, Julie wasn't sure whether or not she should tell her mother about the murder. She hated to upset her but finally decided that even as isolated as her mother was, sooner or later she would talk to someone and find out. And she decided it would be better for her to tell her mom than for anyone else to.

When she got out of her car, tears came into Julie's eyes as she thought about Jane Lucas. It was a lovely day, clear with an invigorating nip in the air. In the light wind, leaves from the big maple in the front yard were falling gently and randomly. A couple of them landed on her, and she could smell, faintly, the sweet smoky leaves burning at a neighbor's house. In the woods, a flock of birds was singing. And she could hear Miller's Creek flow over its stony bed. Before she went in, she thought about how she'd tell Momma about the murder. When she went inside, she went immediately to her mother's bedroom. Bonnie Veere was sitting up in bed reading. She smiled faintly when Julie came in. Julie sat on the bed beside her.

"How are you feeling today, Momma?" Julie said.

"Just fine, dear."

She always said that, no matter how bad she felt, and because of her leukemia, she felt bad most of the time.

"Something terrible's happened, Momma. Jane Lucas has been murdered. It was apparently some kind of cult murder, and people in town are talking about nothing else. Everybody's scared, of course, and we're all hoping the murderer will be caught soon."

Bonnie nodded her head slowly. She looked almost wraith-like in her white silk nightgown and wispy white hair. Since she'd come down with leukemia, it seemed like she'd aged twenty years, and she looked much older than she really was. She was so weak most of the time now, it seemed to Julie like it was hard for her even to raise her hand.

"I'm certainly very sad to hear it. Be sure to tell Mona and Walt how bad I feel for them," speaking of Jane Lucas's parents.

"Of course I will, Momma."

Breda didn't quite go back to normal soon after Jane Lucas's murder, but within a few weeks, it more or less did. Sure there was still quite a bit of talk about it, among the old retired men who hung around the town square on nice days, at the barber shop and hair stylist and at the Holland State Bank, but it quickly became not much more than a conversation piece. Many people actually enjoyed speculating about what had really happened or who might have done it, or what the exact state of the investigation was. A few people in town had become minor celebrities from having been quoted in the *Holland Sentinel* and on WOTV from Grand Rapids and other media in west Michigan. But it soon became the case that the murder wasn't really a pressing concern for most people. Fears that there would be more murders and that Jane's murder might become part of a serial killing faded away in no time at all. The police had determined that the letters written on Jane Lucas's body, *ZOSO*, were related to the rock band Led Zeppelin, so everyone figured there must be some kind of connection to the commune. As a result, the town had decided collectively that if there were any more victims, they'd be people who lived or were associated with the commune. The average citizen figured he or she didn't have much to worry about. You could almost see a palpable look of relief on people's faces a couple of weeks after the murder. The worst thing was the commune had been vandalized, and the people who lived there were more likely to be taunted now when they came into town.

Breda was a pretty smug town, and it returned to its smugness quickly. It was as if the townsfolk said that Breda was the same kind of town it had always been, with the same kind of people. Sure Jane Lucas had been murdered, and they felt bad about it, but when you look at who she hung around with and how she stayed up all hours of the day and night, you'd have to say she took risks you can't afford to take anywhere any more. There were even some folks, like Jack Booth, who thought, I told you so, but even he realized it would be in bad taste to say it. Someone visiting Breda a month after Jane Lucas's murder wouldn't likely have noticed anything different than they would have a month before the murder. The few people who'd bought guns right after the murder would have felt silly admitting it by then. Only a few people, like Jim Leiden, thought about it and worried about it and felt really bad for Jane's family.

Hinton Kurtz laughed when he thought about how safe and secure everyone in Breda was feeling. That would only add to the shock they'd feel when he killed his next victim, and it would make the next killing so much easier. Using a phony name many months before, he'd rented a rundown farm house a few miles outside of Breda. He'd spent those months really getting to know the town and its people. To carry out his Master Plan, that was absolutely essential. He worked as a handyman, so he heard many things about the town and its people from scraps of everyday conversation. Also, he went into town enough so that he could take the pulse of the mood there and hear what people were talking about, but not quite enough so that he'd become well known, and people would begin to wonder about him. Occasionally he hung out at Leiden's Market. Sometimes he'd stop for a drink at the Bucket Inn bar. When people asked him about himself, he provided just enough vague details so that he wouldn't seem too mysterious. Breda wasn't such a big town, and before too long, Kurtz thought he knew it quite well. Of course, he didn't use his real name. Instead, he went by the name Mel Kravitz.

He couldn't help but feel a certain triumph whenever he thought about how cleanly he'd pulled off Jane Lucas's murder. Nobody had the slightest idea who'd done it or why. He imagined the cops pulling their hair out in frustration trying to make sense of it, and he thought what a brilliant move it was on his part to write the Led Zeppelin letters into Jane Lucas's body to throw the pigs off, make them think it was some kind of cult murder. Now, Kurtz thought, the pigs would focus all their attention on the commune, thinking that something like the Manson killings was in the works. Never would they be able to imagine how carefully and skillfully he'd followed Jane Lucas to the party, then waited until she left the party and raced ahead along the route he knew she'd be likely to go home on. He knew that because for weeks he'd been watching her and learning her habits.

Kurtz had his next victim picked out and was ready to carry out the crime. This is the one that will change the town forever, Kurtz thought. There'd be no more forgetting about it in two weeks like everyone had done with

Jane Lucas. This time there wouldn't be one person in Breda who wouldn't feel threatened and wouldn't be constantly worried. This is the one that would start the mass exodus from town. This is the murder that would really give him his first taste of revenge.

Chapter 3

Not many people felt worse about the murder of
Jane Lucas than Bill Mathers, the sheriff of Van Dyke
County. He felt bad that she'd been killed, and from the
bottom of his heart, his sympathy went out to her family.
The murder had also made his job much harder. All of a
sudden, this job that was usually a piece of cake and paid
him $35,000 a year had turned into a pressure cooker. He'd
lost count of how many people had told him that he had
to find the murderer, though he often got the feeling
they didn't even care that much. They just wanted to
needle him. He felt a lot of pressure to try to solve the
case. The pressure from other people didn't bother him
much, though, compared to the pressure he'd put on
himself, because he liked Jane's parents so much and felt
so badly for them, and because he'd been outraged by the
brutality of the crime. There's nothing he would have liked
better than to catch the murderer, but in a way, he felt like
the case was mostly out of his hands. The state police and
the Michigan attorney general's office had gotten into the
act, and their investigators could barely hide their contempt
for his small town way of doing business. They were so
damn patronizing it made him sick. But he wasn't about to

sit on his ass and just let them take over the whole thing. It would be sweet, he thought, if he could beat them to it.

Sheriff Mathers was of medium build, and although he was muscular, he'd gone a little soft in recent years and had a bit of a paunch, and his brown hair was starting to go gray. But his eyes were intense, and you had no doubt when you were talking to him that you had his full attention. The problem Mathers had was he didn't really even know where to start looking for the murderer. He hadn't jumped to the same conclusion everyone else seemed to have about the Led Zeppelin connection. Sure it looked like the Manson murders, but he'd met some of the people up at the commune and didn't think there was a chance in the world they had anything to do with it. Unlike an idiot like Jack Booth, he thought, I know that everyone with long hair and bell bottom pants isn't a crazed murderer. Still, he didn't have any leads to pursue, so he thought he might as well go out and talk to some of the people who lived there. Jane Lucas had spent time at the commune. Quentin and Pursley, the two state police detectives assigned to the case, had questioned everyone there extensively. But Mathers thought he, in his unpretentious way, might be more likely to get the people who lived at the commune to talk than they had. Maybe he'd be able to glean some nugget of information that would lead to something else. And at least he'd have an answer the next time Booth or one of the other assholes asked him about it who thought he should go up to the commune and arrest everyone.

Although he was dressed in casual civilian clothes, Mathers felt funny as he walked up to the old Smith farm house that was the main living area of the commune. This was different than talking to people who lived there when they were in town. This was their turf. He felt almost as out of place as if he were visiting a tribe in New Guinea. The first person he saw was a little kid with long blonde hair playing with a truck out back of the house by the barn. He wasn't sure if it was a boy or a girl, but assumed it was a boy because of the truck. But here that may not mean much, he thought. Though the kid looked up at him a moment, he went back to playing with the truck like he didn't care that Mathers was there. Mathers saw that the letters ZOSO—the same as were found on Jane Lucas's body—were written in red on the side of the gray barn, and a little shudder went through him. He knocked on the door. A pretty, thin girl with blue eyes answered it. She had long blonde hair and was wearing a tie-dyed T-shirt.

"What do you want?" in a voice that was anything but friendly. She only opened the door about four inches.

"I'm Bill Mathers, the county sheriff," he said. "I'm investigating the murder of Jane Lucas. She spent some time here, and I want to find out what people here know about her. Would you mind if I come in?"

"Yeah, I'd mind a lot. Don't even think about it unless you have a warrant. There isn't anyone here that doesn't know less about her than anyone in Breda would," with a touch of anger. "She lived there all her life. She was here maybe three weeks. And the state cops have already been out here and given everyone the third degree."

"There's a guy named Steve Shannon she spent some time with, from what I've been told. What can you tell me about him?"

"He doesn't live here anymore."

"I already know that. I mean what can you tell me about him as a person."

"I could tell you a lot if I wanted to, but I'm not going to tell you a damn thing."

"Look, you may think it's really hip to hate every cop you see," Mathers said. "But by acting like a bitch to me, you may end up hurting yourself or someone you care about. There's an insane killer running free, and for all I know his next victim may be you. I didn't come out here to accuse anyone of anything. As a matter of fact, for your information, I'm one of the few people around here who's been defending this place. Half the people in town would like to see me come up here and throw everybody in jail. All I want to do is catch the killer, and the more information I have, the more likely I am to do that. But if everyone's as hung up on stereotypes of cops as you are, I'll never get the chance."

That got to her, he could tell. He could tell she was surprised to hear him talk like that instead of like the robot image of a cop he thought she probably had in her mind. She opened the door wider.

"I'm sorry, but we've really been getting hassled by people around here, and it's made us pretty thin-skinned. And last night someone painted that *ZOSO* on the barn."

A tall man in a lumberman's jacket with a thick mustache came around the corner. His hair was fairly short for the commune, and he was older than the girl, probably

28 or so, Mathers thought. Unlike the girl, he didn't seem immediately suspicious.

"What's going on?" he said.

"I'm Bill Mathers, the country sheriff. I'm investigating the murder of Jane Lucas. I just want to ask a few questions, and then I'll get out of your way."

The guy, Mike Ferrell, nodded.

"What can you tell me about her?"

"She was a real partier, but seemed like a decent enough person," Ferrell said. "A guy who used to live here, Steve Shannon, met her at a concert, and she ended up coming out here for a while. She wouldn't do her share of the work, though, so we more or less told her she had to leave. Everyone's expected to do their share of the work."

Mathers couldn't help but smile a little. The idea of someone getting kicked out of a commune for not working was amusing to him. The image the straight world had of a commune was of people getting high, screwing their brains out, and listening to rock music all day.

"She was a pretty mixed up kid," the woman, Peggy Lindsey, said. "She tried to act hip, but there was a side of her that showed she was still really like a kid."

"What can you tell me about Shannon?"

"He said he grew up in Southfield, but his folks don't live there anymore," Peggy said. "They got divorced and his dad moved down to Florida someplace, and I don't know where his mom went. I think he said she still lives somewhere around Detroit."

Mathers looked over at Ferrell.

"He never told me anything. He talked to Peg more than anyone else."

"He never told anyone much about his past. People don't here very much. He's a good guitarist. He used to play in a band called The Grim Reapers."

"Were either one of them fans of Led Zeppelin?"

"No more than anyone else," Peggy said.

"You'll be wasting your time if you investigate Shannon," Ferrell said. "He didn't kill Jane Lucas or have anything to do with it."

"She might have told him something, though. He was really the last boyfriend, or whatever you want to call it, she had before she was killed. Why did Shannon end up leaving here?"

"He said his band landed a gig in LA, and they were hoping to go out there and cut an album," Peggy said. "But I think he wanted to leave anyway and wanted to ditch Jane. He didn't really fit in."

"From what I know about the murder, it sounds like it was the random violence of a madman."

"I'm inclined to agree with you," Mathers said. "But I'd still like to talk to everyone who was around Jane Lucas near the time she was murdered. Strange things happen in murder investigations. Sometimes a person you'd never suspect will tell you the clue to the whole thing, and they may not even know themselves that it is."

Thoughtfully they looked at each other. Mathers asked them more questions, but the answers they gave didn't add much to what he already knew. They said they'd let him know if they heard from Shannon or could think of anything else about Jane Lucas they thought might be of value to the investigation. Mathers left with pretty much what he'd expected. A little bit of information about Shannon and the belief that it was highly unlikely anyone at the commune had anything to do with the murder of Jane Lucas. This wasn't like the Manson family by a long shot. They were just a group of people who wanted to try a different way of living, Mathers thought. He was too open minded to have a knee jerk reaction against them or to try to harass them for no reason. And especially not to try to nail them for murders they had nothing to do with.

It was such a beautiful day, sunny and in the 60s, that Evelyn Rijssen had decided to hang her wash up outside to dry. She rarely got the chance this late into October, but in October in Michigan, you really never know what kind of weather you're going to get. A day like this was no less likely than a snowfall, though certainly less likely than those cloudy October days that seem to go on endlessly, where the temperature never gets out of the forties.

It's an oddly quiet day, she thought as she hung the sheets and shirts and pants out on the line. Her husband, Dan, was at a cattle auction in Battle Creek, and the kids were in school, and as isolated as they were out on the farm, she could almost have believed she was the only person in the world. Because she was a farmer's wife and didn't work at a regular job, though, she was used to being alone, and it didn't bother her most of the time. Just on certain days when all of a sudden the loneliness would seem to hit her out of the blue. Sometimes that even happened when Dan was in the house. They'd grown apart since the first years of their marriage, and though they rarely fought and didn't feel much resentment of each other, Evelyn still felt at times they were more like two people who happened to share the same house than like husband and wife. The wind picked up and stirred through the leaves in the woods and on the ground, and Evelyn felt desire stir through her. She wanted someone to hold her.

Though she hadn't heard anyone approaching, she felt suddenly she wasn't alone any more. She turned to see if anyone was around and saw a man walking toward her. She froze for a moment as she tried to recall who it was and as she remembered what had happened to Jane Lucas. She was sure she recognized him but couldn't think of his name. He was walking at an even pace, not running, but didn't say a word. "What do you want?" she shouted.

She turned and ran, but the man quickly caught her and tackled her. Her face hit the ground hard and she could taste dirt in her mouth. She screamed loud as the man turned her over and pulled out a knife. A feeling of horror greater than she could ever have imagined jolted through her. She struggled, but the man was immensely stronger than she was, so her struggle was futile. Then the man thrust the blade of the knife into her throat, and she knew she was going to die. Blood burst out of her throat and all over the ground.

Bill Mathers was sitting at his house after work drinking a Frankenmuth beer and watching Huntley and Brinkley talk about the latest developments in the

Vietnam War. He wasn't really listening to what they were saying, though. It was just background noise for his thoughts. He was thinking about how one of the problems with being sheriff was that people would call you at every hour of the day and night, usually about some piddly ass thing that could easily wait until morning or that wasn't really his job. It made it hard for him ever to really relax. Ever since Jane Lucas was murdered, though, he practically jumped every time he heard the phone ring, fearing that someone was calling about another murder. He wasn't nearly as confident as everyone else in town seemed to be that it was an isolated incident and that the murderer, whoever it was, was now long gone. On the contrary, the more he investigated the case, and the more he thought about it, the more he felt like the killer would likely strike again.

The phone rang as a Buick commercial came on.

"Evelyn's been murdered, Bill," Dan Rijssen said, crying. "You'd better come right out."

Even though he'd half been expecting a call like this, Mathers was too shocked for a moment to even reply. He wondered if he should ask Rijssen anything about the murder and decided not to.

"I'll be right out, Dan, as fast as I can get there," he finally said. "Don't touch anything at the murder site. Once anything's changed, it could be a lot harder to analyze the evidence."

"It's too late, Bill. We already brought her inside."

"Have you called anyone else yet?"

"No."

"I'll call the county medical examiner's office to have them come pick her up. Just sit down and be as calm as you can, and I'll be right out."

When Sheriff Mathers arrived at the Rijssen farm, he went inside the old white farmhouse. The Rijssens' teenage son Rick and daughter Angie, whom Mathers guessed was about eight or so, were sitting in the parlor. Evelyn's sister, Sandy, was there, too, on a sofa with her arm around Angie. Their eyes were red from crying.

"Where is she?" Mathers said.

"Upstairs," Sandy said. "Dan brought her up to their bedroom, and he's in there with her. It's the first room on the right from the top of the stairs."

"I want you to know how bad I feel about this. I'll do everything I can to find the killer."

Sandy nodded, and Rick put his hand up to his face and started crying again. As Mathers walked up the stairs, he felt anger and outrage about Evelyn Rijssen's murder that surpassed what he'd felt about any crime in his whole career. Seeing Evelyn's kids crying and imagining how they felt without a mother filled him with rage.

Mathers opened the door slowly as he walked into Dan and Evelyn Rijssen's bedroom. Evelyn was lying on the bed with a blanket pulled up to her chin. Dan was sitting by the bed holding Evelyn's hand and turned slowly as Mathers came in. Mathers put his arm around Dan's shoulder and noticed the blood on his hands.

"Dan, my heart goes out to you. I'll work night and day if I have to until I find out who did it."

"Thanks, Bill. I know you'll do your best."

Mathers went to the bed and pulled the blanket down to Evelyn's waist. What he saw almost made him vomit. Her face was horribly contorted. There were several jagged cuts in her throat and dried blood all around it. Then he lifted her shirt up and saw the letters *ZOSO* written in blood. Seeing them was so jolting to Mathers he felt like he might collapse. Nothing he'd ever dealt with before in his law enforcement career was even close to this terrifying. He put Evelyn's shirt back in place and put the blanket back over her, and sat on a chair across from Dan.

"Why don't you tell me what happened?" Mathers said, his voice strained, wondering when the state police would arrive. He'd radioed the state police post at Holland on his way to the Rijssens'. He was extremely anxious for them to arrive to take the case over from him. He knew he wasn't capable of handling it alone or maybe even handling it at all.

"I came home from the farm auction up to Battle Creek about five o'clock. The kids were already home, and they weren't too concerned that Evelyn wasn't here, even though her car was here. They just figured she must've went somewhere with one of her friends. Nothing really seemed to be out of place. But when I got home, I just had a feeling something wasn't right. I looked around a little, then I called Evelyn's mom and the only two friends of hers I figured she'd've gone out with anywhere that time of day. And when none a them'd heard from her, I started getting real worried and looking all over the place. Then I saw blood by the clothes line and followed the trail of blood to the edge of the woods. I felt like my mind dropped out of my body. I couldn't think. I was just frozen there like a tree for a minute. Then I thought about Jane Lucas and about started crying. I ran around like a madman to see if I could find Evie. I went into the woods next to where the blood was and sure enough, within two minutes or so I found her, about twenty feet into them. The most horrible sight I've ever seen," looking away from Mathers, trying to keep from breaking down. "Even worse than what you see now, before I cleaned her up."

Mathers thought, I wish you hadn't done that. You may have destroyed any chance we had to get fingerprints.

"The state police and the ambulance should be here any minute," he said. "When they get here, we'll go outside and look at the place where you found her."

Mathers was going to ask Dan a few questions, like if anyone had threatened Evelyn, or if he knew of anyone who'd want to kill her. But he knew it would be futile, that he'd just be wasting words. The murder was as much a mystery to Dan Rijssen, Mathers felt sure, as it would be to a monk on a remote mountain in Tibet.

When detectives Ken Quentin and Mort Pursley of the state police arrived a few minutes later, they examined Evelyn Rijssen's body. They were soon joined by the county medical examiner, who examined the body himself, wrote something on a form, then had his assistants load the body into the ambulance to be taken to the morgue. With that done, Mathers and Quentin and Pursley approached Dan Rijssen.

"I hate to do this to you, Mr. Rijssen," Quentin said. "But I'm going to have to ask you to show us where you found Evelyn's body. There's no substitute for investigating a crime scene right after a crime has occurred."

Rijssen nodded his head like he was only half aware of what was going on around him, and without saying anything, led the three men downstairs.

When they went outside, it looked like there was a party going on. About ten people were milling around by the road and on the lawn. But none of the people in the crowd were members of the Rijssen family.

"What in the hell are all of you doing here?" Mathers said, knowing he'd made a mistake by not staking off the site of the murder the very first thing after he'd arrived.

"I heard about the murder on my police radio and came down," Allen Reusel said.

"I want all of you to get the hell out of here," Mathers said. "What you're doing by tramping around on the lawn is probably destroying any chance we'll ever have to solve Evelyn Rijssen's murder."

"If you do as good a job of solving her murder as you have on Jane Lucas's, I don't suppose it'll matter much," Elaine Shuster said, to some nervous laughter.

That really pissed Mathers off.

"I'm ordering everyone who doesn't have direct knowledge of this murder to leave. In five minutes, I'm going to arrest anyone else who's still here for interfering with a police investigation. And I'll start with Elaine."

There was some grumbling, but the crowd broke up and started to walk to their cars. It was a weird incident that

Mathers would think about for a long time. Later, he'd think it was the first sign that Breda was coming undone psychologically because of the murders.

Dan Rijssen led Mathers and the men from the state police to the place where he'd found the blood and tried to lead them to the place in the woods where he'd found his wife's body. Several state police cars had just arrived. Quentin and Pursley had state troopers put yellow tape that read POLICE LINE - DO NOT CROSS around the area where the blood was found and assigned one of them to stand guard. By now it was getting dark, and each of them held a long police flashlight. Yet it was clear shortly after they started walking that Rijssen was unsure of exactly where he'd found Evelyn. Perhaps it was because of the shock of what had happened or because in the dark so much of the woods looked alike. Also, the trail of blood from the clothesline where the murder had occurred ended. He led them slowly and haltingly and finally stopped at a place just deep enough in the woods that they couldn't see the lights of the house anymore through the trees.

"I believe it was right here," he said, flashing his light over a small clearing covered with dead leaves.

A half moon shone overhead. An eerie silence was followed by a gust of wind that seemed to heighten the bittersweet scent of rotting leaves. There was no blood and nothing to indicate a body had lain there.

"You don't sound too sure," Pursley said. "Maybe you're just too upset by everything right now."

"It seemed like this was it," Rijssen said, his voice breaking some. "It's so hard to tell now. There was a lot more light then. There was blood on the leaves."

"I don't see any here," Quentin said.

"Who the hell knows?" Rijssen said, his voice breaking more. "These woods all look the same from here to the Upper Peninsula."

"We'll come back in the morning with some tracking dogs," Pursley said. "Maybe we'll have better luck then. We'll keep a man posted here to make sure no one goes in and messes anything up."

Shortly after they came out of the woods, a reporter and camera crew from WOTV in Grand Rapids arrived. Mathers recognized the reporter. He'd come to town before to do a story on Jane Lucas. Though WOTV often reported from lakeside resort towns when there was a festival going on or something else of interest, the Jane Lucas story had been the first the station had ever done on Breda, which was somewhat inland and not a tourist attraction.

"I was wondering if I could talk to you guys," the reporter said. His name was Tom Grant. He was young and blonde and handsome, and every hair was in place. He seemed to know Quentin and Pursley.

"How in the hell did you get here so quick?" Pursley said. "You're like a bunch of vultures."

"You have to be fast in this business," Grant said.

"Mr. Rijssen doesn't want to talk right now," Quentin said. Rijssen was walking back to the house.

Pursley didn't like dealing with the press, but he accepted it as part of his job. He'd learned the hard way that the police department owed the public information on important cases. But he liked to give reporters a hard time.

"Why don't you tell me about the murder, and then I'll ask you some questions on film?" Grant said. "You know the routine. I especially want to know if it's related to Jane Lucas's murder."

"The murdered woman's name is Evelyn Rijssen. She was 36, a housewife and mother of a 13 year old boy and an eight year old girl."

He went on to tell Grant what he knew about the case and how there definitely seemed to be a connection to Jane Lucas's murder. Mathers imagined how it would come out on the 11 o'clock news, and he thought about Evelyn. He felt outrage and an overwhelming loneliness, as if everyone around him were speaking a language that he couldn't hope to ever understand, or as if he were invisible to them.

Before long, reporters and cameramen arrived from the *Grand Rapids Press* and the *Holland Sentinel* and a couple of the other TV stations in the area. Now that a second murder had occurred in Breda, the story was about as big as a story could get in that part of the country. They mingled with what had become a small army of police officers.

After what seemed like an eternity to the Rijssens, all the strangers left except the sentry guarding the area where the murder took place: The policemen and detectives, the reporters and cameramen, the medical examiner, the gawkers who slowly drove by. Meanwhile the Rijssens sat in their house together, sharing a grief that no one else could even have imagined.

In the morning, the police found the place in the woods Kurtz had dragged her after he'd murdered her.

Chapter 4

When Jane Lucas was murdered, a few people around Breda had been really scared for a while, and most everyone was at least a little bit worried for a few weeks or so, but the fear didn't last long for most, and after that most people scoffed at the idea that there was anything to be worried about. But after Evelyn Rijssen was killed, a deep, dark fear that was close to panic set in all over town. Most everyone who didn't already own a gun went out and bought one, and some people who already had guns went out and bought more. A few guys built up a small arsenal at their homes, as if they thought the killer might show up at the head of a small army.

People went without sleep, some prayed to God to free Breda from the terrible killer that was stalking it, others started talking about moving away. Like with most things that happened in Breda, Leiden's Store became a place where people from town would gather to talk about the killings. Jim noticed that a lot more people came into the store but that sales actually went down. A lot of people came in to talk who never had any intention of buying anything. It was especially bad the first Saturday afternoon after Evelyn was murdered. As usual, everyone gathered around the wood burning stove, a relic of the past that Jim's family had kept even though the store had long ago installed central heating. It wasn't just for show, though. They used it during the winter, and it saved them money on fuel bills.

"What this town needs is a posse to go up to that commune and look for evidence," Jack Booth said. "Tear the place up looking if we have to. You can't tell me they aren't breaking every law in the book anyway, no matter what Bill Mathers says."

"That's ridiculous, Jack," Jenelyn Robles said. "Haven't you ever heard of the Constitution? There isn't one bit of evidence that anyone up there had anything to do with the killings."

She was redheaded and buxom, with fiery blue eyes. She worked as an office manager at a furniture company in Grand Rapids.

"Oh, yeah?" Jack said. "Jane Lucas was up there all the time."

"I heard she hardly spent much time up there at all," Jenelyn said. "There's probably a hundred people in town she spent more time with than anyone up there—maybe even you."

"If Bill Mathers had any guts, he'd go up there and clean that place out."

"He's got plenty of guts," Jenelyn said. "Enough not to let a bunch of rednecks stampede him into arresting innocent people."

"I ain't waitin' till they find out who the killer is," Harry DeGraaf said. "I'm moving to Holland tomorrow." Everyone looked at him, at least mildly surprised. None of them had heard he or anyone else was actually leaving, although they'd all heard rumors of a mass exodus from town. "I ain't waitin' till my wife or my daughter gets killed to get out."

"What about your house?" Ellen Vriesland said, in a high, whiny, unpleasant voice. She was gray and frumpy and always sounded like she was worried about something.

"I put the For Sale sign up this morning."

"Who in the hell do you think you're going to sell it to?" Ellen said, laughing sarcastically. "The killer?"

"I don't much care right now."

"This town'll become a ghost town if we don't do something," Jack Booth said. "If we don't run those hippies out of here. I still think my posse idea is the best one I've heard yet."

"You sound like those preachers who burned all the witches in Salem or used to act like they wanted to burn people in this town, for that matter," Jenelyn said. "Why don't you go home and read *The Crucible*?"

"I'm announcing a sale," Jim said. "90% off all inventory for anyone who promises not to talk about the murders anymore."

No one seemed to hear him except Jenelyn, who smiled softly.

"I don't know about anyone else, but I went out and bought me a Browning automatic rifle," Keith Ferrari said. "I could put twenty holes in the guy before he even knew what hit him."

"You'll probably end up shooting the mailman," Jenelyn said.

The talk went on and on and nearly drove Jim nuts after a while. The others could leave, but he was stuck there and had to listen to it all day. The cast of characters changed. People would leave, but new ones would soon arrive to take their place. Jack Booth, though, stayed almost all morning. Jim wondered how he'd react if he asked him to start paying rent. It seemed to Jim after a while like he'd heard the same conversations and the same lines over and over again, and maybe he had. But he didn't want to hear any of it. All he could think about was Julie. All he could do was worry about her constantly and wish he could be with her to protect her or just be with her, so he knew she was all right. He couldn't wait until the store closed so he could go out and see her. Today was the day, he decided. He had to talk her into marrying him and moving into town with him to live. Many times he went over the arguments he could use, trying to decide which were most likely to persuade her. He felt sure they could move her mother without any harm and make her feel comfortable at a new house in town. He looked up at the clock. Sometimes that morning, it seemed to Jim like it had stopped. There were still six more hours until the store closed.

When Jim was driving to Julie's after he closed the store up, if anything he was even more apprehensive than he'd been during the day around the store. Especially since he'd called a couple of times and there hadn't been any answer—although he knew this didn't mean much, because Julie often went out and unplugged the phone, so it wouldn't disturb her mother. He just had a feeling something was wrong, and all the talk around the store about the killings hadn't made him feel any better. The billboards he passed in the countryside, advertising the Turkey House restaurant and Pro-Gro Feeds and one that said, "For God so loved the world he gave his only son" John 3:16—and below it the words Breda Dutch Reformed Church—didn't really register with him. Then he turned onto the back road that led to Julie's house, and there were no more signs, just rolling hills with apple trees and grape vines and an occasional farm house and barns. When he finally did get to the house, he saw her yellow Corvair parked out front and Kraut, her German Shepherd, lying on the lawn, and he immediately felt better. Somehow, he felt everything was all right. When he walked into the house, she was there to greet him, and they hugged.

"I've been really worried about you," Jim said.

"Don't be silly, Jim," Julie said. "I'm as safe as could be with Kraut to protect me. He'd mangle anyone who tried to get near me."

"It would only take one shot to neutralize him."

"If the guy ever got that far. Kraut probably wouldn't even let him out of his car. And besides, this killer doesn't seem to be a gun guy. He's into knives."

"Oh, yeah? What if he decides to change his modus operandi? If I had to bet money on it, I'd bet he's got a houseful of guns wherever he lives."

"If it's a *he*. We don't even know that yet."

They were still holding each other and looking into each other's eyes.

"I'm worried about you being out here this isolated. I think about it all the time."

"I wish you wouldn't. You've got better things to do than worry about than me. Everything'll be all right here. Nobody wants to mess with a German Shepherd."

Jim almost asked her if she'd marry him and move in with him right then and there, but he decided to wait until later. The timing wasn't right. To talk Julie into anything, he knew, you had to pick just the right moment.

"Come on in and sit down and stop worrying. I'm cooking lasagna, and I baked an apple pie to boot."

During dinner, Jim tried to act as normal as possible and even tried to be funny when he told Julie about Jenelyn Roble's sarcastic remarks at the store. But he knew he came across flatly and that the humor sounded forced. He was just never going to feel right until either the killer was caught, or Julie moved into town with him.

After dinner they watched *The Sterile Cuckoo* on TV, although Jim had so much on his mind, he barely paid attention to it. After Julie's mother was well asleep, they went up to Julie's bedroom to go to bed themselves. They made love, and to Jim it seemed sweeter than ever before, and he thought he'd never felt so much love for her. He even forgot about the killings, as they told each other again and again as they made love that they loved each other. He never ceased to marvel at her softness and beauty and the passion between them when they made love. He loved her so much. Without her, he thought, his life would mean nothing. He thought he was   the luckiest guy in the world. After they made love, they held each other and kissed for a long time. Then Jim turned on the soft light on the end table by the bed and they lay close and talked.

"God, that felt good," Julie said, laughing. "We ought to do that more often."

"Every day wouldn't be too often for me," Jim said. Now, he thought. Now is the time. "Look, why don't we get married? We could buy a house in town, and you and I and your mom could live together. I understand real estate's going pretty cheap in Breda right now," with a smile.

"Oh, Jim, I don't know," holding him tighter. "You know I want to, but I just don't know if Momma could take the disruption right now."

"I'm worried about her, too. She's not safe out here, and sometimes neither you or Christine is here," referring to the woman who took care of Julie's mother during the day while Julie was working. "I'll never sleep through the night again when I'm away from you, and you and your mom are here alone."

"I really am more worried than I let on. Maybe now is the time for us to get married. Let me think about it and talk to Momma. I'll let you know within a week. You can start looking through the home book if you want," smiling, referring to the local guide of houses for sale. "I really love you, Jim. You've stuck it out with me like no one else would."

She held him tighter, and they made love again. Before he met Julie, Jim could never have imagined he could love someone so much. He was haunted by the fear of any harm coming to her.

Suddenly, Breda was the most famous place in Michigan. The two cult-like murders had caught the fancy of the public, and the press was quick to pick up on them as a Big Story. For a while after the murder of Evelyn Rijssen, it sometimes seemed to people who lived in Breda that there were more reporters and cameramen around town than there were people who lived there. It was hard to walk through town for a while without someone calling out, "Excuse me. I'm Alice Gendelman of the *Holland Sentinel*. Could I ask you a few questions about the murders of Jane Lucas and Evelyn Rijssen?" Or practically the same words would come from someone from the *Grand Rapids Press* or the *Detroit News*, or WOTV in Grand Rapids or WKZO in Kalamazoo.

A few people like Jack Booth and Harriet Erskine loved the spotlight and would talk to reporters for as long as they'd listen. But most people from town were disgusted by the whole thing and wished they'd all go away. It just made it that much harder to put the murders out of their minds and was giving the town a black eye it would likely never recover from.

The raw feelings among the townsfolk were all exposed at a town council meeting that was held the week after Evelyn Rijssen was killed. The meeting room where it was held at the town hall was overflowing with people. As many people were outside the room as there were in it, and more people were probably present than had been at all the meetings the council had held during the past five years put together. The room was brightly lit, and the five members of the council must have felt more like the subjects of an inquisition than the democratically elected representatives of the town. Bill Mathers of the sheriff's department and Ken Quentin of the Michigan State Police were on hand to report on the state of the investigation into the murders. However, the township supervisor, Ted Nyberg, was determined that the meeting would have a semblance of normalcy and tried to begin it with first item on the agenda he had prepared for that night's meeting.

"The first item on the agenda tonight is a proposal to extend a sewer line down Naarden Road," Nyberg said.

The crowd erupted with fury.

"Who in the hell gives a damn about a goddamn sewer line when people are being slaughtered by a madman?" Art Zemlick yelled, pointing at Nyberg.

"What are you going to do, fill it with corpses?" Brenda Surratt said.

"If you try to do anything but discuss the murders, we'll throw you out of this room," Jack Booth said.

"Shut your big mouth, Booth," Marcia Haas, a big, tough, beefy woman who'd been on the council for ten years, said. "You damn Nazi."

Nyberg struck his gavel several times.

"Order, please! Order!" he said, but he looked like a cornered animal. "I move to alter the agenda to begin with the police report on the murders of Jane Lucas and Evelyn Rijssen."

All the other members of the council except Marcia voiced their assent.

"Sheriff Bill Mathers of Van Dyke County and Detective Sergeant Ken Quentin of the Michigan State Police post in Grand Rapids are here to discuss the status of the investigation."

Both men rose and went to the podium.

"We regret to say that we don't have any promising leads yet on the murders," Mathers said. "But we have a multijurisdictional task force investigating them that includes myself, officers from the state police post at Grand Rapids, and investigators from the state attorney general's office. We're also receiving assistance from the FBI."

"How about those hippies up in that commune?" Jack Booth said. "I'll bet they're behind it. Who else would care about Led Zeppelin? I'll bet they got on drugs and murdered Jane and Evelyn just like Manson and his bunch."

Some of the crowd said "yeah" but as many jeered at Booth.

"We've virtually eliminated the people who live at the commune as suspects," Quentin said. "Everyone up there was accounted for during the times of the murders, and no one there had any motive to kill the women. It's as simple as that. All the evidence points to a single, deranged killer."

"Who says they were all accounted for?" Booth went on. "Does that mean you took their word for it?"

"We're satisfied with the proof we have that they weren't there," Quentin went on. "That's all I've got to say about it."

"What are you doing to make sure no one else gets murdered?" Art Zemlick said.

"We're patrolling Breda and the surrounding area 24 hours a day. We've held meetings and gone door to door to explain to people how to protect themselves. And we have the best investigators available working on the case. We think it's highly unlikely the killer can break the blanket of security we've put around this town. We're doing everything humanly possible to protect the citizens of Breda and find the killer."

"Except run that commune out of town," Booth said.

Mathers wished that Pursley had come to the meeting rather than Quentin. He knew Pursley would have chewed off Booth's ear so bad it would have stung for a week.

"We're doing everything we can, Jack," Mathers said. "You don't know what in the hell you're talking about."

"If you knew what you were talking about, the killer'd be in jail right now."

"One more remark out of you, Booth, and I'll have you kicked out of this room," Marcia said. "This is a democratic meeting, not a mob scene."

That shut Booth up temporarily, but others chimed in, and before long, it was obvious to all the council members that they weren't going to get any business accomplished. All they'd be able to do is provide a bitch session for people who were worried about the murderer. They adjourned the meeting and didn't schedule another.

Right after the murders of Jane Lucas and Evelyn Rijssen, townspeople came into Jim Leiden's store in droves looking for other people to talk to about the murders. But there came a point not long after Evelyn's murder where no one wanted to talk about them at all. The subject became so taboo that if anyone was foolish enough to mention them, anyone who was listening was likely to leave immediately or make a remark you couldn't print in a family newspaper.

For Jim, this partly explained why business dropped off dramatically at his store. No one wanted to hear anyone talk about the murders, and a lot of people had gotten into the habit of always shopping outside of town, so as to have another excuse to get away from Breda for a while. The store was losing money, and Jim didn't know how much longer he'd be able to stay in business. It was a marginal business even when times were good.

The store was empty one day when Emil Zeeland came in. He nodded at Jim and walked around the store like he wasn't sure what he wanted to buy or was looking for something, although he knew the layout of the store well enough. Emil was one of the oldest citizens of Breda and had lived there all his life. Jim was surprised to see him come into the store alone. He didn't think his daughter and son-in-law, whom he lived with, would let him go anywhere by himself under the circumstances. Jim wondered if he hadn't got tired of being cooped up in the house and snuck off. He'd lost some of his faculties and become more eccentric in recent years, and Jim wondered if he understood the danger he might be exposing himself to by going out alone—or how upset his daughter and son-in-law might be if they suddenly found that he'd disappeared. Although the two murder victims so far had been women, there was no guarantee that the next victim—if there was one—would also be a woman. Jim decided he'd call them when Emil left to make sure they knew where he was. Emil ended up coming up to the counter with a Hostess Twinkie, a quart of milk, and some Swiss cheese. As Jim rang up the items, he and Emil didn't say anything to each other, nor did they as Emil handed Jim a five dollar bill, and Jim gave him back $1.56 change. They didn't speak as Jim packed the groceries into a bag either. The silence wasn't unusual and didn't feel awkward. It seemed to Jim that he did half his business without talking to his customers now. If anything, the silence had come to feel more comfortable than talking would have.

Jim expected Emil to just pick up his bag of groceries and leave. But instead he stood there and finally spoke up.

"You ever hear about the curse that was put on this town?" he said.

Jim tried to remember.

"I remember hearing kids talk about one when I was a kid, but I never took it seriously after I grew up," he said. "It was just something kids would use to scare each other, and I'm sure a few kids lost some sleep thinking about it. But it was the kind of thing you just laughed at when you got older or forgot about completely."

"It don't sound so funny anymore, does it?"

"I don't know. I probably haven't thought about it in ten years. I don't think the kids today even talk about it. It used to be kids would hear about it from their grandmothers or grandfathers, but the old folks nowadays don't talk about it. Maybe they're not old enough to remember the time when it was still fresh in everyone's mind. I don't really even remember what it was all about any more."

"Well, the story behind it was true. A man named Obadiah Kurtz was hanged outside this town in 1889 for murdering his wife. He didn't kill her nohow, and everybody knew it was a frame-up, but he was convicted anyway. You see, people was afraid of him. He was strange, and people said he'd made a pact with the devil. They said he was practicing devil worship out at his farm, which was probably a bunch of horse manure. But he wasn't a member of the church, and they didn't trust him. In those days, of course, there was only one church in this town, the Dutch Reformed, and if you wasn't a member of it, you was blackballed from everything."

"Where does the curse come in?"

"Just before Obadiah was hanged, he put a curse on Breda. He said someday he'd come back, or his son or grandson would come back, to avenge his death and destroy this town."

"And that's what you think these killings are all about?"

Emil paused for a moment before replying, as if he wasn't sure he wanted to commit himself to an opinion.

"I can't rightly say. I've thought about it, though. I don't believe all this stuff about the rock 'n roll band."

"You haven't said anything to the police about this, have you?"

Emil laughed.

"No, I sure haven't. You know what they'd say."

"Yeah, I suppose I do. Are any of his people still around anywhere?"

"He had a brother, Aaron. Obadiah's three boys and girl went to live with him and his wife. And he had a sister here, too, whose name I don't know. Anyway, the whole lot of 'em picked up and left after Obadiah was hanged. But Aaron only moved to Sand County, to Morrisey, where they didn't have so many Dutch Reformed. Our family has some people up in Morrisey, and from what I hear, Obadiah's son Moses might still be alive, maybe the only one left who can still remember what happened."

"That's a strange story. Of course, there can't really be anything to it."

"I don't know as I'd say yes or no to that. I'd best be going now," and he picked up his little bag of groceries and started for the door.

"Are you sure you want to walk home alone?" Jim said.

But Emil didn't seem to hear him and went out the door. Jim followed and called to him.

"If you want, I can call Emily and have her come pick you up," in a loud voice. "You shouldn't be out alone. It's not safe to be out alone here anymore."

But still Emil didn't seem to hear him or just chose to ignore him. He just kept walking. Back into the store Jim went and called Emil's daughter.

"Emily, this is Jim Leiden. I just wanted to let you know that Emil's been down here at the store. He just left and he's walking down Cherry Street."

"Thank God, Jim!" Emily said. "Barry's out looking for him right now. We've been worried sick."

"He's fine. He was just here and told me a strange story."

"Oh, I'll bet he did. He tells a lot of those these days."

"Hopefully Barry'll run into him. If not, Emil should be home soon anyway. He's headed the right way. He should be safe since he's right in town."

"Who knows if that's even safe anymore!"

Jim hung up, and the eerie silence that had pervaded the store so much lately descended on it again. Only now the silence seemed more complete than usual. Jim found that he couldn't get his mind off Emil's story. It held a fascination for him in a way that a story of that kind normally wouldn't. He laughed darkly as he thought the murders were getting to him just like they were everyone else, and if he were smart he'd forget Emil's story and try to think of anything besides the murders. But suddenly he found it difficult even to think about Julie for long. He kept going over Emil's story about the curse and tried to picture Obadiah Kurtz's hanging. He decided he had to know more about it, and already the thought was forming in the back of his mind that if he could somehow track the whole thing down, maybe he could put an end to the curse and the murders that had occurred in Breda. Maybe he could find out who was committing the murders. If he could do this, he thought—and it was really the only thing that mattered to him—Julie'd be safe, and nothing could happen again that could take her away from him.

He'd think like this for a while, then he'd laugh at himself for it, but the laughter was the kind that nearly brought him to tears. In the next moment, his fixation with the story would begin again, and finally he realized that he'd never be able to rest or feel contentment again until he learned as much as he could about Obadiah Kurtz and his curse on Breda. Tomorrow he'd go to Morrisey and try to track down whatever of Kurtz's people were still around. He'd uncover the secret to the whole thing. And maybe, just maybe, he'd find out who the killer was.

Jim found it hard to think about anything but the story of the curse for the rest of the day, and it kept him from sleeping much that night. One thing he didn't do, though, was tell Julie. That was rare for him, because he usually told her everything, but for now he kept the story to himself. He was afraid it would sound too crackpot, and the last thing he wanted was for Julie to think that he'd been swept up in the hysteria that had so many others in Breda in its grip. He wanted to seem as calm and strong with her as he could be and didn't want to do anything that would make her worry about the murders any more than was necessary—although if anything, she'd probably been handling herself in a more level headed manner than he had.

Even when he and Julie made love that night, Jim found it difficult to keep the story out of his mind. He just hoped his father would be sober enough in the morning to cover for him at the store while he went over to Morrisey. Then he wondered: If I close the store, will anyone even care anymore?

Chapter 5

Jim's father *was* sober enough to watch the store the next day, so Jim drove to Morrisey to see what he could find out. It was a cold, cloudy day with a stiff wind, one of those fall days that give you the distinct feeling it's going to snow. When Jim got out of his car in Morrisey, the wind tousled his sandy hair, and he heard leaves swirling in the street and the crisp sound of branches swaying. He wasn't sure where to start. Though he'd been to Morrisey many times and played football and baseball against their teams in high school, he didn't really know anyone who lived there. It was a town about the size of Breda, only a few miles from Lake Michigan, but there were no good beaches nearby, so, like Breda, the town had never developed as a resort town. It remained a fruit farming town, picturesque in a somber way with its old brick downtown stores, but slowly dying. Its story was the same as Breda's: Not many of the young people stayed there to live anymore after they grew up.

Jim ended up going first into Mott's, a small grocery store. Not many people were in the store. Jim went over to the old man who was at the only cash register that was open.

"Howdy," Jim said. "I'm looking for a man named Moses Kurtz. Could you tell me where he lives?"

The old man looked at Jim suspiciously and didn't reply for a moment.

"He hasn't lived here in twenty years," he said. "He's probably been dead for ten years. I don't think I've even heard his name mentioned in ten years."

"Do you have any idea where he moved to?"

"Seems like it was Florida or someplace warm like that."

"There are still some Kurtzes in town, though, aren't there?"

"Sure, there's a boatload of 'em. An odd kettle of fish, the whole lot. His daughter Annie's here, and some of the next generation, Carmine and Roy, and a bunch more."

"Where does Annie live? I'll try talking to her." The old man gave Jim another suspicious look.

"I can't imagine why anyone'd want to talk to her. She's meaner than a hornet and crazier than a loon. She likes to keep to herself. She was married once but they found her husband hanging from a rope in a closet about five years later. It was ruled a suicide," as if skeptical of that judgment. "She still goes by his name, though. Annie Kurtz Abilene."

"How do I get to her house?"

"Well, lemme think. You go down Blueberry Street this way," pointing in the direction away from the lake, "just about a mile past town till you come to K Drive, then turn left and go about another mile, and then look for a big green house on the right all by itself. There's a gnarled old oak tree out front and a old rotten barn out back with a cow weather vane. Be real careful getting out of your car, though, because she's got about the meanest Rottweiler dog I've ever come acrosst. If he's out in the yard, you may not even be able to get out of your car. If she don't want to talk to you, she sure ain't gonna call him away. And most of the time she don't want to talk to nobody."

"Maybe I picked the wrong Kurtz to try to talk to. Are any of the other ones any friendlier?"

The old man shook his head.

"They're all alike," he said. "They're the nastiest, meanest brood you'd ever want to come acrosst."

Jim thanked the old man and left the store. It had started to snow, a blowing, swirling snow, which added to the eeriness that Jim felt as he drove out to Annie Kurtz's house. Everything surrounding his car seemed to disappear in the snow, and he swore as he thought how difficult that would make it to find the house. After he turned onto K Drive, he slowed to a crawl to make sure he didn't miss the house. As it turned out, though, it was easier to find than he thought. The house was large and Gothic and rundown enough to have been home to the Munsters. Shortly after Jim pulled into the dirt and gravel driveway, he heard the Rottweiler barking, and before he had come to a stop, the dog was beside the car barking at him and looking up at him viciously.

He wasn't sure what to do. He couldn't very well expect to just get out of the car and walk up to the house. Yet he wasn't about to just leave, either. If anything, his curiosity about the curse had only increased on the drive out to Morrisey and his talk with the old man at Mott's. He honked, and hoped—probably foolishly, he thought—that Annie would see he was there and call the dog off. He couldn't even be sure she was home, but there was an old Chevy in the driveway, so he was pretty sure she was. The honk changed exactly nothing. Snow swirled around Jim's car, and when he looked out the window, he still saw the Rottweiler with its paws on his car and murder in its eyes looking through the window and barking.

Jim turned off the rock music station he'd been listening to and thought some more. He wondered what the dog would do if he got out, if he'd really bite him or just bark at him and look mean. He tried to figure the odds and laughed at himself for doing it, then looked around his car to see what he could use to keep the dog at bay or even to hit him with if he really got nasty. He remembered that he still had a baseball bat in the trunk from last summer that he'd never gotten around to putting away. To get to it, though, he'd have to either get out of the car or crawl into the back seat and pull the seat back. He ended up climbing over the front seat and pulling the back seat out to get to the trunk. Then he got out of the car from the back seat on the opposite side from the Rottweiler.

The dog immediately scrambled over to where Jim was, but he held the bat straight out in front of him and kept the dog at bay. It barked viciously and jumped up some but
didn't try to lunge at Jim as he walked backwards toward the house. He finally got to the front door and knocked on it with the large iron knocker. No one answered. He stood there with snow blowing in his face and a barking

Rottweiler that seemed would like nothing better than to rip him to shreds. Yet he could see there was a light on in the house and felt sure Annie was home. Finally, after the third time Jim knocked, Annie Kurtz Abilene opened the door about six inches.

"What do you want?" she said, angrily.

She was thin but looked fit and strong for her age. Her iron gray hair was combed back severely, and she wore wire rimmed glasses and an old fashioned frock.

"Would you please call your dog off, so we can try to carry on a conversation?" Jim said.

She looked like she wasn't certain if she should or not, then opened the door enough to let the Rottweiler in.

"Thank you. I need to talk to Moses Kurtz, who I understand is your father. I was hoping you could give me an address or phone number where I could get in touch with him."

She seemed taken aback, like that was the most outrageous thing anyone had ever asked her.

"He's been living in a nursing home in Ocala, Florida, for twenty years. Why would a young man like you want to talk to him?"

"I want to talk to him about something that happened many, many years ago, and that as far as I know, he's the only one living who could tell me about it. I'm studying the history of this area."

"And what might that be?" her anger seeming to rise.

"I want to learn the story behind the execution of your grandfather."

Her jaw fell, and her face had a look of outrage and anger and perhaps fear, Jim thought, a look unlike anything he'd seen on anyone's face before. She slammed the door.

He stood there for perhaps a minute, wondering if he had said things differently, if Annie Kurtz Abilene would have told him more. But he didn't know what else he could have done, short of making up some outrageous lie that she would never have believed. He walked slowly back to his car, tossed the bat onto the floor of the passenger side of the front seat, and got in. I guess I wasn't cut out to be a detective, he thought, smiling. Yet he *had* learned that Moses Kurtz lived in a nursing home in Ocala, Florida, and later that would mean everything.

As he was driving away he was thinking about what to do next. He decided he'd go back into Morrisey. He'd go to the town library and get the phone book and call some of the other Kurtzes to see if any of them would talk, maybe ask the librarian if he or she knew them. He figured this might be his last chance before Annie talked to them all and got them dead set against telling him a thing.

It had taken a lot of convincing by her, and soul searching on his own part, for Jolene Van Riper to get her husband, the Reverend Larry Van Riper, to leave to go see Johnny Winder at the hospital in Grand Rapids. The boy had been in a terrible car accident the night before, and his family were members of Reverend Van Riper's church. He and his friends had been out riding around and drinking late at night and had run off the road into a tree out in the country. One of the boys, Les Dykhuis, had been killed. Although the driver, Bert Egmond, got off with only a broken nose and some scratches on his face, Johnny had broken both of his legs and his back and ruptured his spleen. He was paralyzed from the waist down, and the doctors didn't know if it would be permanent or not. Reverend Van Riper knew that he should go up without hesitation and see the boy and minister to him and his family.

But although he was normally one of the most conscientious of pastors, he was so afraid of harm coming to his wife from the insane killer who was terrorizing Breda, he'd neglected his pastoral duties lately and would refuse to go out unless she could go with him. The most pacifistic and meek man under ordinary circumstances, he'd become so caught up in the fear and hysteria about the killings that he'd gone out and bought a pistol after Evelyn Rijssen had been murdered. He'd taken lessons on how to use it and insisted that Jolene take them with him. He kept the gun on the end table beside their bed at night and on the counter in the kitchen during the day. He'd practiced and found that he could always get to the gun within five seconds if he had to.

Tonight Jolene couldn't go up to Grand Rapids with her husband. She was taking an art history class at Van Dyke Community College, and there was a test the following day. She simply had to stay home and study. So, very reluctantly, Reverend Van Riper left her at home to go visit Johnny Winder and his family. However, he went only on the condition that Jolene promised to keep the pistol beside her wherever she went in the house—even if she only went to the bathroom.

She made the promise, but with no intention of keeping it. Though she was frightened of the killer and went along with her husband's idea of buying the gun, she didn't share his obsessive fear, and as time had gone on since Evelyn Rijssen's death, she'd become gradually less concerned. If anything, Larry's obsession with the killer had become almost more of a burden to her than fear of the killer itself. At times he would talk of nothing else. He'd go on and on about how bad he felt for Jane Lucas's family and Evelyn's family. He'd spin out theory after theory about who the killer might be and what his motives were. Or he'd talk about what else he could do to make the house more secure or Jolene less vulnerable to attack. He'd already put in an expensive alarm system and helped set up a neighborhood watch program. The only thing he hadn't done was get a dog, but he had an aversion to dogs that even fear of the killer couldn't overcome. Besides, he figured the killer would be caught sooner or later, and then he'd be stuck with the dog.

So in a way Jolene was relieved to have him out of the house for a night. Peace and quiet was in the house for a change that she'd almost forgotten existed. Soon after he left, she made some tea, turned on the radio to a Muzak station, and sat down on the sofa in the living room to relax. She had her books and notes beside her, but she wanted to enjoy the peace and quiet for a while before she got into serious studying. Though she'd put on some weight the past couple of years, she was still quite attractive. Because of her large brown eyes and big lips and thick auburn hair, she looked far too sexy to be a preacher's wife. She had a careless sensuality that she seemed to be unaware of, but that somehow made her even more attractive than if she had been aware of it. She dressed and acted modestly, so people often didn't notice when they first met her how really attractive she was.

Though she felt calm and relaxed when her husband first left, before long, once she started studying, she began to tense up. She started focusing on every little sound, cars going by, gusts of wind, and every little creak and echo in the house. When her cat, Fancy, jumped off the easy chair onto the floor, she started and almost cried out, and a pang of fear went through her. She thought about getting up and getting the gun off the kitchen counter, but then smiled and thought that was just the kind of thing she wanted to avoid, getting caught up in the hysteria the way Larry had. So she let it lay where it was and went back to her notes on Michelangelo and Raphael.

By 10:30 she was done studying and began wondering where Larry was. Grand Rapids was barely a half hour's drive away, and he'd been gone since 6:30. That meant he'd probably been at the hospital for three hours, and she couldn't imagine him staying there that long. The only thing she could think of was that Johnny had taken a turn for the worse. Maybe his life was in danger, she thought, or he'd died. Even if that was the case, it seems he would have called her. Maybe I should call the hospital to make sure he got there all right, she thought. Yet she felt almost strangely frozen into inaction. She felt for a time as if she were glued to where she was sitting, nearly catatonic.

She felt fear creeping into her, like it had been injected into her and was slowly making its way through her bloodstream. Though she'd thought she was above the fear and panic that seemed to have most of the people of Breda in its grip, she realized now that she'd been affected by it just like everyone else, only more subtly. Yet she felt that if she gave in to it, her darkest fear might be realized, and she'd become a victim of the murderer. Maybe that's why she held back from getting up now and getting the gun off the kitchen counter. She stared at it. She could imagine the cold steel in her hand and her finger on the trigger. She even imagined the killer breaking into the house and her shooting him. She just couldn't imagine what his face looked like. So in her mind he was like a headless killer or a killer with a stocking over his face, which was more horrible to her than if she knew what his face looked like.

The wind had picked up, which aggravated Jolene because it made it harder for her to tell if someone was trying to break into the house, made it harder for her to distinguish real noises from phantoms. At times she thought she *could* hear someone knocking at the door or trying to pry the door open, but then she'd realize it was just the creak of tree branches in the wind or some such thing. It suddenly dawned on her that the phone hadn't rung all night, which was very unusual. Rare was the night when someone from the congregation or her mother or her best friend, Pauline, didn't call. Many more people than usual had called shortly after the two murders, looking for spiritual nourishment to ease their fears and sorrow. Maybe the people have even given up on God, she thought. Maybe I should call someone? She almost reached for the phone to call the hospital. But she still felt nearly frozen to her seat.

Then she heard a squeak that she felt certain was someone trying to pry the back door open! She felt like crying, but for a moment longer, she just sat where she was. Finally, though, she bolted from the sofa and grabbed the gun off the kitchen counter. She gripped it tightly in her hand and put her finger on the trigger. She walked slowly to the back door, imagining the horror she'd feel if she saw the gruesome eyes of the killer through the window. She hated the idea of shooting anyone, even him. The awfulness of having him bleeding and slowly dying on her back porch, writhing and moaning like an animal, was more than she thought she could bear. She hoped that when he saw the gun he'd run away, and then she could call the police, and from her description of him they'd be able to catch him.

But when she got to the back door, no one was there. Just darkness and the black branches of trees shaking in the wind, and the swing in the yard creaking and swaying back and forth like ghosts were sitting in it. When the phone rang, it startled her so that she cried out. It was so unexpected that she stood there until it had rung several times before she went over to answer it.

"Jolene? This is Grant Winder. I wanted to talk to Larry. He said he was coming up tonight," sounding irritated.

"He did," her voice quavering, no longer trying to hide her emotions, nearly crying as she said it. "He left here at 6:30. Somethin' terrible must've happened."

"Don't panic, Jo. We don't know anything yet. Call Bill Mathers and see what he knows."

When she started dialing Bill Mather's home phone number, she started crying so hard she had to stop dialing. She hung the phone back up and cried hard. All the tension of that evening, all the fear and stress and tension that she'd suppressed since Jane Lucas had been murdered, came to the surface at once. For one of the few times in her life, she just gave way completely to her feelings. Somehow she knew her husband had been murdered or had been killed in a car accident. She couldn't think of any other possibilities. She cried uncontrollably and thought of what a bitter irony it would be if after all the precautions Larry had taken to protect her, all his worry and concern had been wasted. If all the time he was worrying about her, he should have been worrying about himself. Finally, she was able to compose herself enough to pick up the phone and call Mathers.

"Hello, Mr. Mathers," she said with her Southern accent. "This is Jolene Van Riper. Ma husband Larry left for Community Hospital in Grand Rapids at 6:30 but he never got there."

"I haven't heard of any accidents on the scanner," Mathers said. "I wouldn't panic if I were you. Almost always when people are reported missing, they aren't really missing. Usually there's just some kind of misunderstanding."

"No, Mr. Mathers. Ah'm sure Ah'm raght."

"Tell me which way he went. I'll send some of my men out to look for him, and I'll go out and look myself."

"You know the way he'd go. Down M-45 from our place and down 31."

"Do you have anyone there with you?"

"No. Ah want to go with you. Ah want to hep any way Ah can. If Ah stay here Ah'll just go crazy wonderin' what's goin' on."

"I'm not really supposed to do that. And somebody should stay at your house in case your husband calls. I think you'll be better off staying where you are and having a friend come over to stay with you. But if you really want to go, I might be able to bend the rules."

Actually, if it had been almost anyone else, Mathers would have said no without another thought. It was totally against department regulations to let civilians ride with officers on official business. If anything went wrong, the county could be sued for every penny it had. But he had an attraction to Jolene that was stronger than for any other woman he knew. She ended up getting a neighbor to stay at her house and going with Mathers.

Before long one of Mather's men found Reverend Van Riper's car along a wooded section of M-45 between Breda and Mennon, and Mathers and Jolene and the other deputies Mathers had assigned went there. But though they searched half the night, and called in the state police, they couldn't find a trace of the good reverend. The tracking dogs the state cops brought in couldn't follow his scent more than five feet. The only conclusion that made any sense was that someone in another car had gotten Van Riper to pull over and that, forcibly or otherwise, he had gotten in the other car and been driven away. The police put out an All Points

Bulletin on him and hoped someone would spot him, but there wasn't much more they could do that night.

Mathers ended up taking Jolene back to her house and coming in with her. She made coffee and tried to keep from sobbing. They sat on the sofa in the living room.

"I'll keep my men working on this case around the clock," Mathers said. He couldn't help noticing how lovely Jolene's eyes were, even though he felt embarrassed and guilty.

"Ah know you'll do everything you can," Jolene said. "Ah can't tell you how much Ah appreciate your hep."

No way was Mathers going to tell her what he really thought: That there wasn't a two cent chance that Reverend Van Riper would ever be found alive.

"I told my men to let me know the minute they find any new information, no matter what time of day. I'll let you know what I hear."

"Thank you so much," almost breaking into a sob.

"Is there someone you could call to come stay with you tonight, or somewhere I could take you?"

"Ah don't have any folks in town. Ma folks are mostly in Louaville, Kintucky. Ah met Larry when he was goin' to Bible college there. Ah think Ah'll call my mother and have her come up and stay with me."

Mathers finished his coffee and got up to leave.

"Thanks again, Mr. Mathers," Jolene said. "You've been so kind."

"Call me any time at home or at the sheriff's office, day or night, if you want to find out what's going on or just want to talk."

She pressed his hand.

"Ah surely will."

As Mathers walked out to his car he had the funniest feeling. It was a mixture of the eerie, dark feeling he had about the murders of Jane Lucas and Evelyn Rijssen and the disappearance of Larry Van Riper and the extreme attraction he had for Jolene Van Riper. He imagined the outrage there'd be in town if Van Riper was never found and he ended up taking up with Jolene. But he knew he shouldn't even be thinking about it and tried to block her out of his mind.

Kurtz had never felt such a feeling of triumph and power in his life. He'd pulled off what he saw as another perfect murder, and he didn't think the cops had the slightest idea who the murderer was or what the motive was. He thought what fools they were compared to him and had such an inflated sense of his brilliance, he thought there wasn't any murder he couldn't commit without being caught.

Somehow, revenge against Breda had become the focus of all the hatred and violence Kurtz had inside him, even though he'd hardly even been part of the family. His father, Erich, had been stabbed and killed in a barroom fight when Kurtz was still a baby. He had no memory of him. His mother, Wilhelmina, had been killed in a car accident when Kurtz was six. He'd spent most of his growing up years in a series of foster homes, where he'd been beaten and neglected and become hardened and violent. He'd developed a violent streak that could only be satiated by killing. He started killing animals, and when he'd been caught slitting the throat of a cat when he was 14, he'd been put in juvenile home for a year. But until the Breda killings he'd never killed a person before. When he was nine he'd lived in a foster home in Breda for a year. The kids at school taunted him unmercifully because he was an orphan and because of his slightly deformed left arm. They had no idea he was the great-grandson of Obadiah Kurtz. Hinton Kurtz had come to hate Breda with an intensity that would have shocked even the other Kurtzes had they known.

The only good memories he had were of his loving, barely remembered mother now long gone, and of his grandfather Moses, whom he'd lived with the summer when he was ten. It was Moses who'd told him the story of how Obadiah Kurtz had come to be murdered in Breda. That's how the grandfather had always said it. MURDERED. Obadiah hadn't been sentenced to die. He'd been murdered. Murdered by the town of Breda. And no one there had ever been made to pay—until now.

The idea for the murders had begun with a strange dream Kurtz had one night, where Obadiah had come to him dressed all in white and told him he, out of every other person in the world, had been chosen to carry out vengeance on Breda. The next morning, he started planning the murders.

Chapter 6

Reverend Van Riper's body was found a week later. Chet Bolles and his son Rich were out hunting rabbits early one morning when their English setter ran ahead of them, stopped by the body, and barked. It was a hideous thing to see. His face was contorted into an expression more gruesome than anything Bolles had seen as a Marine in Vietnam. Van Riper was naked from the waist up. On his stomach, Kurtz had written ZOSO in blood, just like Bolles had seen in the paper as having been found on the bodies of Jane Lucas and Evelyn Rijssen. The body was crawling with insects.

Unfortunately, Rich saw the body before Bolles had had a chance to keep him away, and he'd ended up throwing up and crying. Bolles's own reaction might not have been better if it hadn't been for the year he'd spent in 'Nam, where he'd seen so much mangled and bloody human flesh that he'd become numbed by the sight of it, as if he were watching it on TV. He'd been able to make it seem in his mind like it was unreal. If he hadn't learned to do that, he knew he never could have made it over there. Or would have ended up like the guys who were homeless on America's streets, whose brains were too fried by the tragedy of what they'd seen to go on with a normal life.

The reaction of Breda to this latest murder was different than it had been to Jane Lucas's and Evelyn Rijssen's murders. Unlike the hysteria that had followed Evelyn's murder, the reaction this time was much quieter. It was like the citizens of the town had become deadened from fear and loathing. Instead of wanting to talk about it with anyone who'd listen, most people this time wouldn't talk about the murder at all. Many townspeople just made quiet preparations to leave. Hardly any more weapons were sold at the gun shops in the area. Almost everyone already had a full arsenal, but even if they hadn't, they probably wouldn't have bought more guns. Most people had given up hope that having guns around the house would protect them if the killer really wanted to get them.

A dozen families left within a couple of weeks of Reverend Van Riper's murder, and almost everyone else talked about leaving. Most of the people who lived at the commune left, too. They were tired of harassment and scared of the killer like everyone else. Most people who left town just abandoned their houses. There wasn't a chance in the world they'd sell them before the murderer was caught, and the posting of a For Sale sign had little effect other than to provoke the blackest kind of humor. Even people whose families had lived in Breda since it was founded in 1849 thought about leaving.

A bleak, numbing terror settled over Breda, and the reporters who came to the town in increasing numbers only added to the nightmarish quality of it. One of them had dubbed the murderer the Breda Killer, and the name had stuck. They became like ghouls or demons after a while, or the gatekeepers of hell. The town was coming unglued.

Scholars who study mass psychology would have found it interesting to study Breda. After this latest murder, a neurosis bordering on psychosis seemed to grip the town. People would jump at the slightest unexpected noise. Some people carried guns with them constantly like cowboys from the Old West. You heard of people who'd never owned a gun in their life sleeping with one under their pillow. Many devout people lived in Breda, especially among the older generation, and some of them spent hours on their knees praying to God to protect them from the killer. As time went on and the killings increased, people's behavior became stranger and stranger. Things like people who'd been teetotalers all their lives becoming heavy drinkers and straight-laced, respectable women sleeping around indiscriminately. It was something like what happened in medieval towns that were struck by the plague, where moral values collapsed in the face of the horribleness and life destroying force of the disease. Even the strongest people were becoming frayed around the edges psychologically. And everybody had the same question on their minds:

Who would be next?

Jim Leiden was at home watching TV with Julie when the news about Reverend Van Riper was broadcast on a bulletin that interrupted the show they were watching.

"The murdered body of the Reverend Laurence Van Riper of Breda was found this afternoon in a wooded area of a farm near Denton," the WOTV reporter announced from the newsroom. "Police have reason to believe the murder is related to the murders of Breda residents Jane Lucas and Evelyn Rijssen. The same letters, ZOSO, associated with the rock band Led Zeppelin, were found written in blood on the body. Tune in at 11 for a full report."

"How horrible," Julie said. "I don't know if I can stand this anymore."

After much soul searching, Julie had finally agreed to move in with Jim, and they'd rented a nice old wooden house in town. They had decided to wait before marrying, though, until a happier time after the Breda Killer was caught. Julie's mother had made the adjustment well, as always without complaining.

"You have to wonder how many people are going to be left in this town in a month or so," Jim said. "I may have to leave myself if business at the store falls off much more."

Julie moved close to Jim, and he put his arm around her.

"I don't even know what to say anymore," Jim said. "I've run out of words to describe how terrible these murders are."

"What are we going to do, Jimmy? I can't very well ask Momma to move again."

But Jim had just remembered something important, and he hardly heard what she said.

"That name, Van Riper. It just rang a bell."

"Sure, you knew Larry Van Riper. You've known him forever."

"I know. But I was thinking of something else." He remembered that Van Riper was one of the names that he'd run across when he'd gone to the library to research the murder of Obadiah Kurtz. He still hadn't told Julie he was investigating Emil's story about the curse. But he hadn't planned to keep it a secret forever and decided that now was as good a time as any to tell her.

"Did you ever hear the story of a man named Obadiah Kurtz, who was executed in Breda for murdering his wife back in the 1800's?" he said.

"I remember hearing kids talk about it when I was a kid. It was supposed to be some big scandal that no one was supposed to talk about. But I haven't heard anyone mention it in years. After most everyone died who could still remember it, people lost interest. What makes you think of that now?"

"Because I've been doing some checking, and I'm pretty sure there's a connection between that and these killings."

"How so?"

Jim told her about how Emil Zeeland had come into the store one day and told him all about Obadiah Kurtz. He told her how he'd gone to Morrisey and talked to Obadiah's granddaughter, gone to the library to read the account of the murder of Obadiah's wife and his trial in the old *Breda Courier*, and talked to the oldest people in the Cedar Hills Nursing Home in town.

"That's fascinating," she said. "Why didn't you tell me before?"

"I guess I was afraid that it would make you dwell on the murders more, or that you'd think I was starting to lose it like so many other people in this town."

"Don't be silly! Have you told the police about it?"

"No. I was afraid they wouldn't buy it, that they'd just think I was nuts. They're totally fixated on the Led

Zeppelin angle anyway. I want to have a more solid link first. Maybe this is what I need. I'm going to go back to the library tomorrow and go over those articles again. Although Mrs. Beecher is already beginning to think I'm a little crazy for wanting to read all those old papers."

"Oh, Jimmy!" hugging him. "Maybe this can solve the whole thing, and everyone can go back to trying to live a normal life again."

"I'd like to think so. But don't get your hopes up too much. There's still a lot of blank spaces to fill in. Even if there is a link, there's a lot of Kurtzes around who could have done it. And the story's so bizarre, I'm not sure I'll ever be able to get the cops to believe it."

"I don't know, Jim. I think they're desperate right now. I think they'll jump at anything that sounds even halfway plausible. They're under a lot of pressure to do something, and they don't seem to be getting anywhere."

"I hope you're right, Jules. I sure hope you're right."

The next day Jim got his father to mind the store again so that he could go to the library. Al Leiden was spending more and more time lately at the store. Though the opposite might have been expected, the murders and panic in Breda had caused Leiden to drink far less than he had before. He'd been scared into sobriety. He was afraid that if he got drunk, he'd let down his vigilance and perhaps end up being murdered or that someone in his family would be murdered.

The Breda Public Library was empty as usual when Jim went inside, except for old Mrs. Beecher at her desk behind the counter. She looked up and squinted through her spectacles when Jim came in.

"Well, hello, Jimmy," she said in her old woman's voice. "Don't tell me you've come back here to look at old newspapers again."

"I sure have," Jim said, smiling. "I've really gotten interested in learning about the history of Breda lately."

The whole thing was awkward, because he wasn't about to tell her what he was really there for, and he was almost the last person she'd ever have expected to want to study the history of Breda. In a town like that, it was the kind of thing that only old women were interested in, like the women in the Breda Historical Society, who'd sit around drinking tea in their nice dresses at the meetings of the club.

"You know where they are now. You don't need my help anymore."

Jim was quickly able to find the yellowed old copies of the *Breda Courier* containing the articles on the arrest and trial of Obadiah Kurtz. There were no articles about the execution, which wasn't surprising since it was illegal— Michigan had been the first state to ban capital punishment. Sure enough, just as Jim had remembered, one of Obadiah's chief accusers was a Van Riper, Reverend Pieter Van Riper to be exact. He knew he'd remembered right, but he wanted to see it in black and white again to make sure he hadn't deluded himself. This time he wrote down all the names in the story and a summary of it in a notebook he'd brought along. He wanted to start taking a scientific approach to the investigation. He couldn't be sure this Van Riper was an ancestor of Larry Van Riper—it was a relatively common Dutch name—but it was something to go on. Now the obvious thing to do was study the genealogy of Larry Van Riper and Jane Lucas and Evelyn Rijssen to see what connections there might be between them and Obadiah. Jim knew that would be a more difficult undertaking. He wasn't sure if the birth and death records he'd need were in the library—he figured he'd probably need to go to the country courthouse for that—and even if they were, it would be a pain in the ass to get them from Mrs. Beecher. But he felt if he could prove all three of the people who had been murdered were descendants of the people who were responsible for the execution of Obadiah Kurtz, he could confidently go to the police and expect them to at least half believe the curse was the key to the murders. Maybe that would be all they'd need to break the case.

He read the articles again as he thought the situation over. The look and musty scent of the old papers made an indelible impression on him. He smiled as he imagined himself going to Mrs. Beecher and asking her what documents they had in the library related to the genealogy of the people in Breda, and he hoped she wouldn't come over to him and check on what he was reading. He decided the smartest thing to do was to ask how he could trace the genealogy of his own family. At least then he'd know where the material was at. He finally got up and went over to her.

"Mrs. Beecher, you know another thing I've gotten interested in lately is genealogy. Is there anything in here I could use to trace my family tree?"

She wrinkled her brow, even more than she had when he'd asked her about the old newspapers.

"Well, you're becoming an inquisitive man now that you're grown up. I'm glad to see it. Or maybe you're just trying to get your mind off these horrible murders." From somewhere she got a handkerchief and brought it to her eyes. "It's all so awful. Half the time I'm afraid he's going to come in here and murder me next. I've even thought of asking the town council if I couldn't just shut the library down for a while until the murderer's caught. But I suppose people need books more than ever now. If I let the library close, I'd feel like I was contributing to the death of Breda. And it seems like there's so little left now."

They looked at each other. It seemed to Jim that she'd forgotten his question. Then suddenly she seemed to remember.

"You'll have to go to the county records office for birth and death records, Jimmy. We don't keep them here."

"All right then," Jim said. "I'll go there."

He closed his notebook and got ready to leave.

"Come back any time, Jimmy. It's nice to have some company around here."

She smiled her crooked smile in a curious way, and Jim thought she seemed sad and courageous.

In less than an hour, Jim was at the county records office and had the records he was looking for in front of him. Fortunately, he thought, he didn't know the clerk there, so he didn't get hassled about why he wanted to look at the books or get stuck in a long conversation. The records were in binders, with one binder for each decade showing births, deaths, and marriages.

Before he started, Jim thought it would be a mammoth job to go through all the books to trace the family histories of the people who were responsible for the hanging of Obadiah Kurtz. But when he found how few people had lived in the Breda until fairly recently, he decided he might be able to do the whole job in a day or so.

He had the books piled on a table, every one since the county began keeping records in 1839. He read the names of every person who'd been born in the county since the first Dutch settlement. The handwritten yellowed pages of the older books were hard to read because of the archaic handwriting styles, but Jim quickly became engrossed in what he was doing, and the difficulty of reading the names hardly bothered him at all. He constructed family trees in his notebook of Sheriff Jacob Feikema and his deputy Christen Postma, who'd arrested Obadiah and hanged him, Judge David Aacker, who'd tried him, and Reverend Pieter Van Riper, who'd led the crusade and fired up the town to persecute Obadiah. After a couple of generations, he had to use several sheets of paper for each family because some of the people had had ten children. At first what he found out made him want to shout. As he'd suspected, Larry Van Riper was a direct descendant of Pieter Van Riper. He was his great grandfather. And Jane Lucas was the great great granddaughter of Sheriff Feikema.

When Jim was constructing the family tree of Judge Aacker, though, he came across a name that stopped him dead: Julie Veere. She was the great great grandniece of the judge. Somehow when he'd started this business it hadn't occurred to him that he might end up with Julie's name—or his own—on what he called his Death List. How could he have been so naive? Somehow he'd blocked out of his mind the possibility that anyone he was really close to would end up on the list. Now that he had to put Julie's name down, he wasn't sure he'd be able to continue. For the longest time, he sat there thinking about the consequences of what he was doing. Now what would he do? Should he tell her, so she could consider leaving town or take extra precautions to protect herself? Or should he keep it a secret to keep her from panicking or worrying about it day and night? Hadn't she already taken every precaution she could anyway? It didn't take him long to realize it was out of the question not to tell her. She already knew what he was doing, and the next time he saw her, the first thing she'd ask him was whether she was on the list or not. It made him feel a little better when he thought that the two victims he'd linked so far had been direct descendants. Julie was only a great great grandniece. Would that matter to the killer? Or would he only be interested in direct descendants? Questions like that kept eating away at him as he continued preparing the Death List. He wondered if he'd ever be able to sleep again or do anything productive until the Breda Killer was arrested. An eerie feeling went through Jim when he suddenly realized that the killer at some point must have done exactly what he was doing now—checking out Breda's birth and death records from the time of Obadiah's hanging until the present.

Jim ended up with a list of 53 descendants of Reverend Van Riper, Sheriff Feikema, Deputy Postma, and Judge Aacker who were alive and still living in the county. His own name wasn't on the list, but that didn't surprise him, because he knew his own family history well enough to know he wasn't descended from any of the four directly responsible for the hanging of Obadiah Kurtz. He took some comfort from the fact the list was fairly large. It reduced the odds against Julie being killed. But that didn't make him feel much better. The others on the list were mostly friends and neighbors and acquaintances he'd known all his life. Now he had the terrible responsibility of knowing they were possible future murder victims. A shiver went down his spine when he'd completed the Death List and looked it over. He was filled with a terrible doubt. Should he tell his story to the whole town and set off a panic among all the people on the Death List? What if his theory turned out not to be true? Should he tell the police and turn the Death List over to them and wash his hands of the whole thing? Or would they just laugh at him? In a way he'd never anticipated, his investigation into the murders had turned into an awesome burden.

There was another problem, too. He hadn't been able to establish any connection between Evelyn Rijssen and the four men he knew so far were responsible for persecuting Obadiah Kurtz. It made him think there either must have been another player involved that he wasn't aware of yet—or that his theory was wrong. He really hoped his theory was wrong. He thought himself a fool for having got involved in the investigation in the first place—but there was no turning back now.

Jim was filled with dread and doubt as he waited for Julie to come home that day. When she did come home, he told her the story of the Death List without telling her that her name was on it.

"I don't know what to think, Babe," she said when he'd told her the story. "I'm thrilled and horrified at the same time. If you want my advice, though, I say tell the police. Go talk to Bill Mathers. He's someone you can trust who you know won't laugh at you. He'll know what to do."

"You're right. I think I'll do that. But I just want to check out one more thing first. I want to take another trip to Morrisey and try to talk to some other Kurtzes. Then I'll go right over and talk to Bill Mathers."

"You still have Evelyn Rijssen to fit in somewhere, too."

"What I figure with her is there's someone else involved who I don't know about yet, maybe someone on the jury or something like that. I'll have to do some more research to find out."

"But the most important question of all is one I'm almost afraid to ask. Are you or I or Momma on the list?"

"I'm not on it and your Momma's not on it, but I'm very sorry to say you are."

She looked like she'd just heard the most interesting and bizarre thing she'd ever heard in her life. She looked like she was trying to decide what it really meant to her, but she didn't look fearful.

"Well, only one out of three of us. It could have been worse," laughing darkly. "So what should I do? Move to Outer Mongolia?"

"The good news is you're only a great great-grandniece, and Jane and Reverend Van Riper are direct descendants. Maybe that's all the killer's interested in. Or maybe my theory's full of shit since Evelyn's not on the list anywhere."

Jim and Julie were sitting on the sofa in the living room. She moved closer to him and brought her hand up behind his neck and gently massaged it.

"It's wonderful that you're doing this, Babe. I just hope you don't get yourself in any trouble."

"Forget about me. It's you I'm worried about. The whole reason I got into this is you, hoping the killer could be caught before anything happens to you."

"I know. I know you'd do anything for me." She was whispering now, and they were holding each other close. "We need to get our minds off all this for a while."

She unbuttoned one of the buttons on his shirt and put her hand in. Jim put his arm around Julie and caressed her side and breast.

"I'm not sure that's possible."

"It'll be fun to try, though, won't it?" laughing softly.

"We've got nothing to lose, anyway," Jim said, and kissed Julie on the lips, and in a moment, they got up and went into their bedroom.

Jim called his father that night and again asked him to run the store the next day, so he could go back over to Morrisey and try to talk to some of the Kurtzes. Before he left town, he stopped at the store to make sure his father had it open and was sober.

"Just thought I'd stop by and see how things are going," Jim said to Al Leiden, who was standing behind the counter of the store. Mr. Leiden had a cup of coffee in his hand. The scent of the coffee mixed with the smell of fresh copies of the *Chicago Tribune* and the *Grand Rapids Press* that Al had brought in and laid on the counter.

"Like usual these days, no goddamn business," Al said.

"I'll be back in the afternoon sometime. I can take over then if you want me to."

"Whatever you want. I ain't goin' nowhere. Don't matter to me."

Jim wasn't entirely sure if his father was sober or not. He had a glazed look in his eyes, like he might have been drinking, and was talking in short sentences like he often did when he was drunk. But it was usually hard for Jim to tell for sure if he was drunk—unless he really went on a bender. Al Leiden was good at holding his liquor. Whether he was sober or not, though, Jim supposed he could take care of the store for a while.

"What the hell do you want with all this time off lately?"

"I can't say right now. I'll tell you some other time. But believe me, it's important."

"Well, it must be pretty damn important if you can't tell your old man."

"You'll understand why when I tell you later. I'm not sure you'd even want to know."

"Suit yourself. It don't matter to me."

"I'll see you later, Pop. Take good care of everything."

Jim had what he thought was a brilliant idea. He'd go to the Sand County records office and trace the Kurtz family like he had the families of the men who'd been responsible for the execution of Obadiah Kurtz. That way, he thought, he'd be able to find out which members of the family might still be living in the area without having to go around town asking people and getting everyone suspicious.

As it turned out, the records clerk was a cute blonde who looked at Jim like she thought she knew him. He wondered where he might have known her from. She looked a little like one of Morrisey's cheerleaders from when Jim played basketball, he thought. She didn't give him a hard time about letting him look at the records. In a few hours, he'd made up a list of descendants of Obadiah Kurtz who were born in the county. With the list in hand, it was just a matter of looking up the names in the phone book. He went to a phone booth in town.

The first two people he called, Ransom Kurtz and Jackie Stenfors, hung up on him as soon as Jim mentioned Obadiah's name, even though he didn't mention anything about the murders or even say he was from Breda. There was no answer at the homes of the next two people on the list. Jim stood in the cold and isolation of the phone booth as the phone rang on and on. He thought it would make so much difference if he just knew one person in

Morrisey well, someone who really knew the town and could tell him the stories that every town has.

He thought the best place to find a person who'd talk to him about the town, like in most towns, would be a bar. The Black Maria looked like a local bar to the core. Jim went into it and sat down at the bar next to an older man, who had a draft beer in front of him and was talking to the bartender. He thought the guy looked like someone who liked to sit in a bar and talk. It was barely four o'clock, and the bar was practically empty. It was a small, dark, comfortable place, with well worn tables and booths and a juke box in one corner with "The Color of the Blues" by George Jones playing on it. The bartender, Roy, looked tough, with a scar on one cheek and wavy hair that was slicked back. He had distant, cruel eyes that made Jim think he was mocking him.

"What can I get you?" he said.

"Bring me a Stroh's draft, and—" Jim looked at the menu on a plastic sign on the wall behind the bar. "A Black Maria burger with everything on it."

The bartender turned away to pour Jim's beer into a tall glass. Jim didn't say anything to the guy beside him at first. He thought it would be better to let him do most of the talking. He wanted to avoid making him suspicious and maybe have him clam up.

"What brings you to Morrisey?" he said.

"I run Leiden's Store over in Breda. I came in to pick up some feed at Edmonds," which was a feed wholesaler in Morrisey.

The man, whose name was Guy, nodded. It must have seemed plausible enough. Then it must have hit him about the murders. He turned around on his stool and looked right at Jim.

"You're really from there, huh? It must be pretty scary right now."

"It's as bad as you probably think. Most people are so scared they look like robots when they're walking down the street. Half the people are talking about leaving and a lot of them already have."

"I wouldn't even think you could keep a store going there anymore."

"Things have gotten pretty bad. We're not making money anymore. I'm not sure how long we can hang on. I may end up leaving myself."

The bartender had put the hamburger on the grill and had come back to where they were. He made Jim nervous. He seemed to be listening carefully to their conversation.

"This ain't nothing against the people who live there," Guy said, "but I wouldn't live there now for a million bucks. I always thought it was a nice little town, too." Then he turned toward the bartender.

"Bring me another draft, will you, Roy?"

"Another Stroh's for me," Jim said. "And a shot of whiskey on the side."

Jim was nervous. He needed something to calm him down, though he rarely drank much, and because of his father, drunkenness disgusted him. But everything was different now.

"Yeah, I wouldn't live in Breda now for a million bucks," he repeated, louder this time. "How does anyone ever get any sleep?"

"A lot of people don't get much anymore."

"How come everyone hasn't up and left?"

"A lot of them, they wouldn't know where else to go. It's the only place they've ever lived. And the rest don't have the money."

"If it was me, I'd move to Alaska or Hawaii, as far away as I could get."

The bartender put the drinks in front of them and hovered around them. Jim wished he'd at least say something or that someone would come into the bar, so he'd have to go wait on them.

"Has there been much talk here about the killings in Morrisey?"

"Are you kidding?" Guy said. "That's all anyone's been talking about. We ain't that far away. People are scared as hell that Morrisey'll be next. And even if they weren't, this is the biggest story to hit the area in twenty years."

Jim looked away and took a drink. The next question was inevitable. He tried to imagine how they'd react.

"Has there been any talk about the curse on Breda?"

"Curse?" Guy said. "What in the hell are you talking about?"

"A man named Obadiah Kurtz was hanged in Breda in 1889. Just before he was hanged, he put a curse on Breda that he said would be carried out by his children or grandchildren."

Jim waited for him to say something, but he just stared at him. His eyes were riveted to him, though, like he was fascinated by the idea.

"After the hanging, Kurtz's family moved to Morrisey. Some of his people are still here apparently."

"Kurtzes, huh? They're a weird bunch," winking at Roy. "They keep to themselves, and it don't take much to piss 'em off. I wouldn't have anything to do with them myself." But he said it with a bit of a smile. "It just so happens that Roy here is part of that clan. His momma was Myra Kurtz."

Jim felt like he was frozen to his seat. The most unexpected thing he could ever have imagined had happened, and he had no idea what to say next. He was afraid to look into Roy's eyes, he was afraid to speak, yet he felt like he had to say something. The silence was unbearable. But all the things he could think of to say seemed like they'd only make the situation worse. It flashed across his mind that Roy could even *be* the killer.

"So you really think there's a connection between the murders and the Kurtz family?" Roy said, with an undertone of anger. Jim didn't answer immediately, so Roy went on. "Do you think we're Led Zeppelin fanatics or something?" with a taunting smile.

"I didn't say I believe there's a connection between the murders and the Kurtz family. But some of the older people in Breda probably do, who were alive closer to the time Obadiah Kurtz was hanged. To most of the younger people it's just a superstition."

"But not to you, right?"

"You heard what I said. The cops would probably laugh if anyone brought it up to them."

"I don't know about that. I'll bet they'd follow right up on it. I'll bet they'd jump at anything right now. I used to be a cop, and I can tell you, you wouldn't believe the pressure there is to solve a big case. They've got reporters and relatives, everybody questioning them all the time. They're heroes if they can solve it, and everybody thinks they're idiots if they don't. So they'd probably even look into your dirty little theory."

"It's not my theory."

There was an uneasy silence. Jim avoided eye contact with Roy, but he could feel him staring right through him with his cruel eyes. He knows what I'm up to all right, Jim thought.

"Well, I'd better get going. I've gotta get back to Breda. I'll pay my bill now."

"You haven't eaten your burger yet," Roy said.

"I'm leaving anyway."

Jim took a five dollar bill out of his wallet and handed it to Roy. Roy didn't take it at first but finally did and turned away toward the cash register to make change. The metallic sound of the keys of the register and the coins rattling were clear and menacing to Jim. Roy put the change on the bar in front of Jim, and Jim put it in his wallet, leaving a 2 cent tip.

"Thanks for the great service." Then Jim turned slowly in his seat and walked away.

At first, he felt immense relief when he walked outside into the light snow of a late winter afternoon. He felt a bit of panic momentarily when he couldn't remember where he'd parked his car, but he soon spotted it just down the street. He laughed darkly. Who in their wildest imagining, he thought, would have thought the bartender of the Black Maria tavern was one of the Kurtz family, for Christ's sake? Although the more he found out about the Kurtzes, the more of them there seemed to be.

He felt more certain than ever that the curse really was behind the murders in Breda, but the hard evidence was thinner than a spider's web. He wondered how he could ever have been so stupid to go investigating the murders on his own. He was as vulnerable as he could be, with none of the protections the police have. Can there be any doubt, he wondered, about who the next victim will be? Or maybe the Breda Killer would make it twice as painful, more painful than he could imagine, by killing Julie first.

Snow mixed with sleet was falling, a miserable hash that made it hard for Jim to see more than a few feet in front of the car, and at first there didn't seem to be any other traffic. Then, suddenly, Jim noticed there was a pick-up truck right behind him, ridiculously close considering the slippery conditions. Jim thought at first it was Roy and wondered what he had in mind. But then he wondered how he possibly could have left the bar that quickly and started following him. Who'd take care of the bar? Roy had seemed to be the only employee there, unless there was someone in the back room. Or had he called another one of the Kurtzes and told him to rush out and follow Jim on the road to Breda? As hard as Jim concentrated when he looked out the back window, he couldn't tell for sure who was driving the truck. Through the sleet and snow, he could see headlights about six feet behind him and that was all.

Then the pick-up pulled out like the driver wanted to pass. Jim thought that even if Roy or another Kurtz wasn't behind him, he couldn't take a chance and let the truck get beside him where it could run him off the road. So he sped up as much as he could and still stay on the road. The pick-up fell back some, but then speeded up and gained on him. At that point, Jim wasn't sure if it would be more dangerous to try to go faster or take his chances on possibly getting run off the road. Led Zeppelin's "Dazed and Confused" started playing loudly and eerily in Jim's head, and he couldn't get it to go away, even when he played another song on the radio. The snow and sleet seemed to let up a little, and Jim speeded up again, and the pick-up fell back. A car was coming in the other direction, so the pick-up was forced back into the lane behind Jim. Jim tried to calculate how many miles it was and how long it would take him to get Oxbridge, the next town along the road, and what he'd do when he got there. He was scared, but he felt a certain exhilaration about the challenge of trying to get away from the truck, and then he laughed as he thought the person behind him was probably some little old lady who was just trying to pass. But he wouldn't have put much money on that, and he wasn't about to take any chances.

A bar and a store and a bank were in Oxbridge, Jim remembered, and he figured he'd probably be safest in the bank. There'd be an armed guard there, and Roy or whoever it was probably wouldn't try to mess with him. The worst place to go would be the bar, the Bloated Goat.

People would think nothing of a fight in there, he thought. Oxbridge was a tough town, and he'd heard there were fights in the Bloated Goat all the time. If he could just hold out for three more miles or so, he figured, he'd be in Oxbridge and safe. The snow and sleet picked up again, becoming more snow than sleet, and visibility was down to almost zero. Once again, the pick-up pulled out beside him, so fast that the truck was almost parallel with Jim's car before he could do anything about it. This guy must be crazy, Jim thought. Someone could be coming the other way, and he'd never see him until they crashed, and the other car's bumper was down his throat. He could feel his tires starting to slip and thought that if they hit anything more than a slight curve, he'd be off the road. He tried to concentrate totally on the road, but he thought of Julie, too, and "Dazed and Confused" still played in his head like a broken record. He imagined himself getting run off the road into a tree, and Julie sitting at home wondering where he was.

Somehow he managed to stay just slightly ahead of the truck, and then he figured there was probably less than a mile before they'd hit the outskirts of Oxbridge. He tried to look for lights up ahead through the snow but could see nothing. He wondered if he'd miscalculated the distance. He got to a point where he thought he had to be in Oxbridge by now, but still there was no sign of it. Then he felt a certain panic and wondered if he even had the road right, or if he'd somehow got off on the wrong road because of the snow and was out on one of those country roads that never seem to end. The road kept getting curvier, and several times he went a few feet off the road. Once he missed a tree by about an inch.

The road seemed to go on and on like a road in a nightmare, in an empty world that just had a car and a pick-up truck and an endless, snowy road in it. Jim felt certain now they were not on the road to Oxbridge. At times he thought he could see who was driving the pickup, but the face was in shadow. There just wasn't enough light to make out the face, so there was no chance of telling who it was. The Doors' song "Riders on the Storm" came on the radio and mixed with the "Dazed and Confused" playing in Jim's head, along with the sound of his engine whining and the slick turning of the wheels on the icy road. He felt like he was starting to lose it, that his perception of everything was becoming unglued. The exhilaration he'd felt for a while was gone and had been replaced by a fear that seemed to permeate every cell of his body. He even thought of just stopping and having it out with the guy, except he figured the guy was sure to have a gun or some other weapon.

Then just when he thought he couldn't take it anymore, he could just make out the lights of a town shining dully through the snow and the falling dusk. A couple of other cars were coming the other way, and the pickup behind Jim fell back. Jim couldn't tell at first, but finally he started recognizing buildings and knew he was in Oxbridge. When he got to the Oxbridge State Bank, he pulled over to the side of the road, jumped out of the truck, and ran to the bank without looking back to see what the driver of the pickup would do—which he figured would only slow him down. What he hadn't figured, what he'd been too rattled to consider, even though it couldn't be more obvious, is that it was already past five, and the bank was closed. So he ended up pulling at a locked door, on a building that had only a couple of dim lights on in the background.

He almost panicked. He turned and expected Roy (or whomever) to be right behind him. He was almost overcome by fear. But when he looked around, he didn't see any sign of either Roy or his truck. There was a pink neon sign shining over the Bloated Goat and bright lights at the Shell station about a block down the street. He saw a guy walk into the bar on the other side of the street, and on Jim's side of the street, in the other direction, a young couple was walking toward him, talking and holding hands, not even seeming aware Jim was standing there and acting like they were oblivious to the storm. He wondered if Roy was hiding somewhere, and he tried to imagine where. But then he had an even worse fear: That the chase hadn't even really happened or that he'd grossly exaggerated it in his mind. That he was just becoming so unglued by the terror of the murders and the gruesome responsibility of the Death List, that he was starting to lose his mind. That thought gripped him with a panic almost as bad as what he'd felt when he thought Roy Kurtz or whoever it was trying to run him off the road. If he really was being followed, he thought, why wasn't there any sign of the truck when he'd stopped and looked up and down the street? An icy fear gripped his mind, and he didn't even realize how cold he was getting standing outside in the snow. He wasn't dressed at all adequately to be outside.

He also felt a tremendous emotional and psychological exhaustion, like he could have collapsed in the street and started crying uncontrollably. But he kept himself outwardly composed as he stood in front of the bank for a long time, like he was frozen on the spot, frozen into inaction by exhaustion and fear.

Then it hit him how cold his hands were getting, so he blew on them and rubbed them together and put them in his pockets. The fear subsided. He was able to start making sense out of things again. He could feel the snow coming down and hear the wind in the trees. He could smell the wet slushy odor of the snow and the pleasant smell of ground beef and other food smells coming from Avery's Restaurant across the street. He'd forgotten it was even there, and he laughed as he thought it would've been the ideal place to go into. But he didn't want to go into anyplace now. He didn't want to talk to anyone.

Jim got back into his car and started driving home. This time there was no truck behind him, and he thought again how the truck chase seemed half unreal, like the whole day had for that matter. He had no proof that the guy in the truck was Roy Kurtz or any other Kurtz—he didn't even know for sure if it was a man. If it really was Roy, why didn't he just hide somewhere and follow him when he got back in his truck? But Jim thought Roy would probably figure that Jim wouldn't leave town if someone was still following him, that he'd just stop and call the police somewhere where a lot of people were around. The trauma of the chase had been severe enough for Jim that he wasn't even sure what color the truck was or the make. So it was just like another figment from nightmareland, like the scene in the bar. It could even be true that the driver of the truck was just some demented farm kid, and by bizarre coincidence he'd chased him down right after he'd left the Black Maria just for kicks.

Jim thought whoever was in the pickup truck might be waiting down the road for him out of town, that the person would know the road to Breda and wait for him a few miles down, when the protection of Oxbridge was far behind, but Jim didn't worry about it much, and it didn't happen. He'd almost got to a point beyond fear. He kept his radio off. He'd heard enough music for one day.

"How did it go?" Julie greeted Jim when he got home.

"You wouldn't believe it," Jim said.

"That bad, eh?"

"Let's put it this way. For a while I wasn't sure I was going to make it back at all. And then when it was over, the whole thing seemed so strange it was hard for me to believe it even happened."

"Oh, Jimmy!" hugging him. "What happened? You can't make a statement like that and then not tell me what happened."

"I'll probably tell you, but not right now. I'm not sure I've ever felt more worn out in my life. One thing I will tell you right off is that I'm going to tell Bill Mathers tomorrow about my theory. I can't chase this thing alone anymore. It might not be good for my health," smiling a little.

"Well, sit down and relax. I've got some Sloppy Joe mix on the stove. I was wondering if you were ever going to get home."

"I was wondering the same thing myself."

Chapter 7

Mabel Valden had been lonely ever since she'd moved out of Breda to the family's cottage near Ludington. Most of her friends and family were in Breda or thereabouts, and she missed them terribly. She hadn't wanted to move. The last thing in the world she wanted was to move. But her son Alex had been so hysterical with worry about her all the time that she'd finally acquiesced to his plan to move her away from Breda and the Breda Killer. He'd wanted her to move in with him, but she'd vetoed that idea. She wanted to be independent and not in her son's way all the time. It was a comfortable life. She had a charming cottage on Lake Michigan to live in and a housekeeper to take care of things and keep an eye on her during the day. She'd made a good friend in Mrs. Winston, who lived next door and whom she liked to play canasta with and take walks with on the beach. She had plenty of knitting to do for her grandchildren, and when she was too tired to work, she had a nice color TV to watch and a big tub she could soak in. But it wasn't home, and she was lonely most of the time.

She hadn't been worried about the Breda Killer at all. She'd probably worried less about him than anyone else in town. She thought the last person in the world he'd want to kill would be a 75 year old woman in poor health, who probably wasn't going to live much longer anyway. And she wasn't afraid of death anymore. She'd had a good life surrounded by family and friends and laughter. Tears and tragedy there'd been, too, but she had many wonderful memories. She believed in God and heaven. What more consolation could a person have at her age as they faced death? The only thing left she wanted was to move back home to spend her final days near the people she loved the most. She'd decided that she was going to call her son and insist that he move her back to Breda. She could even move back to her old house because nobody'd bought it yet.

She lay in bed thinking about it in the middle of the night. She wasn't sure what had woken her up—maybe it was nothing at all—but suddenly she heard a slight scraping sound. Actually, it was a loud scraping sound, but no sound was very loud to her when she had her hearing aid off, and she didn't wear it to bed. When the scraping sound didn't go away, she started getting scared. In theory, she hadn't thought she'd be scared even if confronted by the Breda Killer. But the more she thought about it, the more she realized how much life still meant to her, how terribly sad it would be if she never got to see her grandchildren again or never got to see another sunset. She heard footsteps and saw a dark figure at her door.

"Who is it?" she said in a fearful, old woman's voice. "What do you want?"

But she got no answer. She sat up as Kurtz came to her bed and put a knife to her throat. She grabbed his arms to try to stop him, but her attempt had no more effect on him than if she'd hit him with a feather. She let out something like a scream, but the sound was weak to begin with and fell off before it could really even get out. Then there was nothing for Mabel Valden. Kurtz turned on the light next to the bed, tore open Mabel Valden's nightgown, and dipped his left index finger in her blood before writing the telltale letters on her waist. He wore a rubber glove so there would be no chance of leaving a fingerprint.

He allowed himself to smile. He'd brought a completely new twist to his murders, and once again, he thought, I'm one step ahead of the pigs. They were so stupid, and he was so clever. What chance did they have of ever catching him? And now there'd be a new level of terror in Breda. Now everyone would have to realize that it wouldn't do a bit of good to try to move away!

It wasn't until after Alex Valden had called his mother on the phone for a couple of days and got no answer that he really started to worry. At first, there was no reason to worry. He'd felt a tremendous sense of relief after he'd moved her out of Breda. After worrying night and day that she'd be the next victim of the Breda Killer, he'd finally been able to sleep at night again.

After two days he'd called his mother's next door neighbor, Mrs. Winston, but she said she hadn't seen Mabel Valden or talked to her. She thought Mabel had gone visiting somewhere. She went over and knocked on Mabel's door but got no answer. So Alex called the Mason County police to go check on her and immediately left for the cottage himself. Officers Handy and Wilton had to break the lock on the front door to get in. They didn't notice until later that someone had jimmied the lock on one of the windows. When they went into Mabel's bedroom, they saw two rats with blood on their snouts scamper away. They found Mabel lying in bed just where Kurtz had left her.

"Oh, fuck, she's dead," Lucas Handy said to his partner Ben Wilton when he saw Mabel. "What a fuckin' mess. How in the fuck did those rats get in here?"

The rats had been eating the corpse. Only the Z in *ZOSO* was left, and the whole area around it, the body, the sheets, and even part of the floor, was covered with blood.

It was by far the most gruesome thing Wilton had seen in this, his first year on the Ludington police force. He felt like he was going to puke, but he tried as hard as he could to hold it back. He'd never live it down back at the station if he threw up.

"Go back to the car and radio the station what happened and have them send Doc Napier here right away," Handy said.

Wilton was glad for the chance to get away, but just as he was about to leave, he took one more look at the body and noticed something.

"Look at this, Lucas," he said, leaning over and pointing at the red Z. "It looks like the letter Z. I'll bet the Breda Killer killed her."

"That could be anything," Handy said. "The fuckin' rat probably did it. And besides, Breda's a hundred miles away."

"It's not a cut, it was written. I wonder where the fuck she's from?"

"Get out to the car! Do you think I want to stand here looking at this corpse all day?"

Fortunately, they were able to get Mabel Valden's body out of the house before Alex arrived. When he got to his mother's house, her body was already safely at the county medical examiner's office, and Deputy Wilton was standing at the door. Other officers were standing around, and a small fleet of police cars was parked in the driveway and on the street nearby. Wilton had been dreading this moment, but he was glad to get it over with.

"All right, what's happened?" Alex said. "I'm Alex Valden, Mabel Valden's son."

Wilton paused before replying, even though he'd rehearsed this scene a hundred times in his head. He knew there was no sense trying to varnish anything.

"I'm sorry to have to say, Mr. Valden, that your mother's been murdered."

Alex didn't say anything for a long moment as the enormity of it and as the folly of his having brought her up to Ludington to live sunk in.

"How could that possibly have happened?" he said and then pointlessly, "She lived in Breda, and I moved her up here so she'd be safe."

A shudder went through Wilton as he remembered the Z he'd seen written on Mabel Valden's body, and the scrap of conversation he'd had with Handy about it.

"We don't have any idea yet who did it or what the motive might be," Wilton said. "But it doesn't look like anything was stolen. Why don't you sit in the squad car, and I'll have someone take you to the medical examiner's office? They'll want you to provide positive identification of the body. And there'll be a doctor there who can give you a sedative or whatever else you might need."

But Wilton got the impression that what he'd said didn't even register with Alex.

"Let me by," Alex said. "I've got to go in and call some people."

"I'm sorry, I can't let you do that. This is a crime scene. Anything that's disturbed might impede the investigation."

Alex, who was normally the most aggressive and self-confident of men, became meek as a lamb. So many thoughts were running through his mind he couldn't concentrate on anything. He was utterly in a state of shock.

"All right. Whatever you say."

Wilton put one arm around Alex, and with the other softly took hold of his elbow and led him to a squad car.

"I want to tell you personally how bad I feel about this, Mr. Valden," he said. "I know how bad I'd feel if it was my mom."

It didn't take long for the police to put two and two together and conclude that Mabel Valden was yet another victim of the Breda Killer. Quentin and Pursley from the state police and Bill Mathers rushed to the scene. Before Mathers joined the official investigation, though, he stopped to see Alex Valden at the Holiday Inn, where he was staying until arrangements could be made to ship his mother's body back to Breda for burial.

Alex came to the door of the room, and Mathers said hello and nodded but decided he'd let Alex speak before he said more. Mathers had known Alex all his life because Alex had grown up in Breda, but he'd moved to Grand Rapids after he'd graduated from college and had become a successful businessman. Mathers hadn't seen much of him since then. They sat on a sofa that faced a window that looked out over the beach to Lake Michigan.

"Why would anyone want to kill her, Bill?" Alex said, a strong note of desperation in his voice. "Why would anyone want to kill a 75-year-old woman who never harmed anyone in her life?"

"I haven't got an answer for you," Mathers said. "Apparently, whoever did it is trying to prove that it won't do anyone in Breda any good to try to move away. And for some insane reason, he decided to use your mother to prove it."

"It's all my fault. The last thing she wanted was to move out of Breda. She never would have come up here if it wasn't for me."

"There's no sense blaming yourself. You did what you thought was right. If she hadn't come up here, he might have got her in Breda."

"I guess you're never ready for a thing like this, are you, Bill? No matter how much you think you are."

Mathers shook his head. "No, you never really are."

Once again, Kurtz thought, he'd pulled off a perfect crime. He'd heard around town that the cops still didn't have the slightest bit of evidence as to who'd killed Jane Lucas or Evelyn Rijssen or Reverend Van Riper or now Mabel Valden. He had to laugh as he imagined how everyone in Breda would react if they knew he'd walked right among them without their having any idea he was the killer who'd ruined their lives. That their innocent everyday talk and gossip had given him all the information he needed to choose and find his victims. He tried to imagine the looks on their faces if they found out he was the Breda Killer, as they'd remember the times they'd talked to him, how he'd been in their houses, how easy it would have been for him to murder them. How horrified they'd be! And no matter how jaded or deadened they thought they'd become after all the murders, the final act of the Master Plan would wake them all up again in a hurry.

He thought about this as he sat by the window of the old farm house he lived in, looking out at the bleak snowy night and the black tracery of the trees and listening to the wind howl. Everyone in town will be terrified now, he thought. No one will feel safe. He'd killed them young, old, middle-aged, women and a man. No one could say they were safe anymore because the killer only killed women or only killed people who were young or old. And nobody anymore could have the comforting thought that all they had to do to get away from the threat is move away. Mabel Valden's murder had ended that. Now they'd all have to think there was NO WAY OUT. Now everyone would be ready to crack from fear and anxiety and wondering if they'd be next.

Sheriff Mathers was sitting in his office daydreaming about Jolene Van Riper. There were a lot of times now when Mathers couldn't focus on his work. The pain and frustration he'd felt because of the murders at times made his mind numb—at least as far as doing police work went. He could have a ton of work to do and not even be able to begin it. So he'd just sit at his desk doing nothing. Mathers never seemed to get tired of thinking about Jolene, even though it made him feel guilty, and even though he doubted he'd ever have the guts to make a play for her. Even if he waited a respectable length of time before he asked her out, it would still be a real scandal around town. Besides, her folks wanted her to move back to Kentucky, and from the way she talked, it sounded like she might do it.

On the other hand, Mathers had got the feeling Jolene had a lot of bad feelings about Paducah and that she didn't want to go back there. She'd said her mother would never let her live her own life when she was there. He figured she probably just didn't know where else to go. There was really no place for her in Breda anymore with her husband dead, he didn't think, and it was a town no one wanted to stay in anymore. But it was the only place besides Paducah she knew anyone.

That kind of thing was running through Mathers's mind when Jim Leiden walked into his office. Jim had had to wait a few days to tell Mathers his theory about the murders because Mathers had been up in Ludington dealing with Mabel Valden's murder. Mathers's frustration with trying to solve the murders had lately turned nearly into resignation that he never would solve them. He'd completely run out of theories about how to go about finding the killer, and it was so painful to think about the killings, he often just tried to block them out of his mind.

Instead of each murder adding to the chain of evidence that could be used to solve them, each one only seemed to make the case more baffling a mystery. If the killer were ever going to be caught, Mathers thought now, it would be by the homicide investigators from the state police or the attorney general's office, with their high tech equipment and experience, not him. However, he did have one big advantage over them: He really knew the town and the people. And it's people, he thought, not equipment or training or experience, that are the most important thing in solving almost any crime.

"What can I do for you, Jim?" Mathers said from the swivel chair behind his desk. "Have a seat."

"I think I'll do that," Jim said, sitting down in front of the desk.

It was a bland, sparsely furnished office. After Mathers had divorced, and his ex-wife had taken the kids and moved to California, in his bitterness he'd taken down all the pictures of his family, and he'd never put any of them back up. A few framed citations were hanging on the faded institutional walls, some pictures from sheriffs' conventions, and a picture of a duck flying over a marsh. His desk was made of gray metal and looked old but was about all a sheriff in a county of 31,217 people could expect.

"So what's on your mind today? Are you going to tell me who the Breda Killer is?" with a touch of bitter irony. There was a meaningful pause before Jim replied.

"I might," and there was a certain gravity in his understated tone that made Mathers immediately take him seriously. Mathers brought his hands back from behind his head and sat up straight.

"You said that like you meant it."

"I'm serious. I think there's a connection between these killings and a curse that was put on this town in 1889 by a man named Obadiah Kurtz."

"I remember hearing about it when I was a kid. But it wasn't the kind of thing you took seriously once you grew up—unless you were pretty superstitious or a little nuts."

"Jane Lucas, Larry Van Riper, and Mabel Valden are all direct descendants of people who were responsible for hanging Kurtz. There's probably a connection with Evelyn Rijssen, too. I just haven't figured it out yet. I did some research and came up with a list of all the possible victims according to my theory."

He pulled out the Death List and handed it to Mathers. He went on to tell the whole story, of Emil Zeeland coming into the store and telling him the story, of his trip to Morrisey to talk to Annie Kurtz Abilene, and his encounter with Roy Kurtz.

"That's really interesting, Jimmy," Mathers said when Jim had finished, as he perused the Death List. "I'll definitely look into this."

Jim was relieved that Mathers didn't act like he was nuts or laugh him out of the room. But he knew also knew that Mathers was a pretty slick politician. He was elected, not appointed, so he needed to be nice to everyone who could potentially vote against him, whether he thought they were off base about something or not. He wondered how much of it Mathers really believed. He seemed to be treating it pretty coolly.

"So you think Roy Kurtz is the killer?" Mathers said.

"I don't know if it's him or not. Maybe he just knows who did it and is covering for them."

"How does this fit into the Led Zeppelin angle?"

"It doesn't. I think that's just a diversion to get people to think it's like the Manson killings and throw all the suspicion on the commune. But you and I both know it's not very likely anyone up there did it."

Mathers nodded.

"Just between me and you, Jim, I'm going to pursue this a little, see what I can find out. But I'm not going to say anything to the state police or anybody else just yet. And I want you to promise me you won't talk to anyone about this or tell anyone you came here to talk to me. If this really is the key to the killer, the last thing we want is for him to know. And sure as hell don't go around showing this list to anyone. It could set off a panic."

"I won't. Things are bad enough around here already. I just wonder how long it will take the Kurtzes to find out exactly who I am."

"They've probably already figured it out."

"It might not be a bad idea for me to get out of town for a while. Dad's been taking pretty good care of the store lately."

"Where do you think you'd go?"

"Florida. I might go to Florida and try to find Moses Kurtz."

Yes, he'd try to find Moses Kurtz—the only living person who could remember Obadiah Kurtz's hanging. Jim figured he had to go somewhere if he didn't want to get killed or get Julie killed. So why not go somewhere where he could help solve the murders? He felt like he was running out of time if he wanted to save Julie and save Breda.

Kurtz sat in his rundown house and thought about it over and over. A guy from Breda might be onto the murder plan. He'd found that out from his cousin Roy when he'd gone up to Morrisey for a visit. Not that he didn't want everyone to find out sooner or later—he wanted more than anything for everyone in Breda to know that the horror that had struck their town was caused by a Kurtz. It's just that it was too early. He didn't want it to get out until he'd destroyed the town beyond where it could ever recover. He figured if it all ended now, in five or ten years everything would practically be back to normal, except for people who'd lost someone in their immediate family. There'd be a new generation of kids who'd hardly know or care what had happened. No, that wouldn't do. The utter destruction and devastation he had in mind wasn't even close yet. Only the death of the town could in some measure satiate his hatred for Breda and the desire he had to avenge the murder of his great grandfather.

The desire had only grown as he'd gotten older, until it seemed to burn in him night and day. How many times had he imagined Obadiah's execution in his mind, and the taunts he'd had to bear right to the moment of his death? More times, it seemed to him, than all the minutes that had ticked away in his life. And as time had gone on he'd embellished the story, as it had been embellished countless times before it was told to him, until the injustice of it seemed more than Kurtz could bear. Until in his mind the great grandfather he'd never known became something like a saint. And Kurtz remembered, too, how *he'd* been taunted as a boy in Breda, how the other kids had teased him until he'd run back to the foster home crying. But Breda was paying now, and they'd just begun to pay. The accounting wasn't even close to being even yet. There were still so many yet who hadn't been struck.

A logical person could have argued that the vengeance was ill placed, that no one left in Breda had anything to do with hanging his great grandfather. You could have argued that most of the people in town weren't even related to any of the people who'd lived in Breda in 1889, but they were all being made to suffer. But thoughts like that never entered Kurtz's head, and there was no one around to make him consider them. Even if someone from his own family had tried to talk to him reasonably about the matter, he probably wouldn't have listened to them. It had become a personal, deranged obsession with him, and nothing anyone could say would have made him change his mind one iota. All the violence inside him had focused on that one idea.

The best part about it, he often thought, was that he was living practically in the midst of Breda, and no one suspected that he was behind the murders. He'd been using a phony name, and no one there knew who he really was. It had been twenty years since he'd lived in Breda as a boy, and he didn't look anything like he had then. When he'd first come back to town, a few people had looked at him like they had a flickering moment of recognition, but he could tell they didn't really know who he was. This anonymity allowed him to savor the suffering that Breda was going through. Every time he went into town, he heard people talk about it or could see on their faces their anguish and fear and loss of sleep. And he heard a lot when he was in stores or hanging out at the Bucket Inn or working on people's houses.

Kurtz wanted to kill one or two more people in Breda, drag out the terror, the hell that the town was living through, before he delivered the final blow that would destroy the town forever and make it a ghost town: Blow up the elementary school and wipe out every kid in it. But now there was a guy who could potentially wreck his plans, who was out on a personal witch hunt looking for the killer. I've got to get rid of the guy, Kurtz thought, and fast. He didn't really know much about him so far except that his name was Jim Leiden, and he owned Leiden's Store. He'd luckily found that out because Jim had given his real name that day he'd gone to the Black Maria. He didn't know where he lived or how he might be vulnerable. But he'd find out. Then it would just be a matter of luring him into a death trap.

Chapter 8

After Jim Leiden left his office, Mathers thought for a long time about what Jim had told him. He tried to figure whether it was just some crackpot notion or whether there could really be something to it. He was aware that he'd become somewhat unhinged himself by the murders and the pressure he'd been under to find the murderer. He wanted to make sure he didn't just jump on the idea without giving it a lot of thought first. If he made a big deal out of it and there turned out to be nothing to it, he could virtually get laughed out of his profession and out of the county. No way was he going to run out and tell the state boys about it, even though technically they were supposed to be working together. Instead he'd make some discrete inquiries on his own first and see if there was anything he could sink his teeth into. Actually, he'd thought briefly about the curse after the murder of Evelyn Rijssen, but he'd rejected it as too farfetched. He hadn't given it any thought since.

The problem would be finding some way he could look into Jim's curse theory without being really obvious about it. He'd have to work on that. In the meantime, he decided to stop by and see Jolene Van Riper.

"Well, what a nice saprise," Jolene said to Mathers in her soft Southern accent when she answered the door. "Come on in, and Ah'll git you a cup of coffee."

"Thanks," Mathers said. "I was passing by and thought I'd stop and see how you're doing."

"Ah've been doin' a lot of work at the church to keep busy," Jolene said as they sat on the sofa in her living room drinking coffee. "Ah've been plannin' all the suppers and makin' food and workin' with the kids a lot. The more Ah do, the easier it is to get ba."

"I know the feeling."

He really wished that he was religious, that he might be able to use that as a wedge—as ironic as that seemed—to get close to her and become more a part of her life. But he hadn't darkened the door of a church in ten years other than to go to weddings and funerals.

"Have you given any more thought about leaving town?"

"Some, but maybe a little less lately. Ah feel lak they really need me at the church to keep people's spirits up. And Ah've really been a hep to the new pastor, Reverend Olander, he says, learnin' about the congregation and where everything is. If Ah just up and left, maybe the other members wouldn't have the courage to stay eitha."

"I certainly hope you stay." He wondered whether he should tell her that, so he made a joke out of it. "If everyone leaves, there won't be anyone to pay my salary anymore."

She laughed. He thought she'd never looked lovelier. It isn't just a matter of lust anymore, is it, he thought? I'm in love with her.

"Ah'm glad someone in this town still has a sense of humor. Most people seem to have lost theirs."

"If I lost that, I think I'd lose my sanity with it."

"It makes me feel better to have you stop ba sometimes. It makes me feel safer. And Ah get so lonely sometimes."

They looked right into each other's eyes. It was all Mathers could do to keep from moving over to her side of the sofa and throwing his arms around her. What's she trying to tell me? he wondered. Is she just making small talk, or is she trying to lead me into something?

"I'm trying to keep in regular contact with all the families who lost someone. I think everyone in Breda feels pretty lonely these days," Mathers said. "Everyone seems to have crawled into their own little world."

"Ah suppose they have. It's a shame, because this is when everyone needs each other the most."

"It sure is."

Mathers took another sip of coffee, but the taste hardly registered. He was completely captivated by Jolene, especially her huge brown eyes, which seemed to draw him toward her like a magnet. He decided he'd better leave, before he did something that would spoil the moment and that he might regret later. He wanted to stay and tell her all about the investigation and what he thought about it. But he decided he'd better get out of the danger zone.

The timing wasn't right yet for him to try to make their relationship anything other than business and neighborliness.

"I'd better be running along now," he said, getting up. "I'm still on duty, and I never seem to get all my work done anymore."

"Are you sure? You haven't finished your coffee yet."

He hesitated before replying, "Yeah, I've got to get back to my office. Until these murders are solved, I feel guilty if I'm not there practically around the clock."

They stood close together by the door. Jolene looked up into Mather's eyes. Does she have any idea what she's doing to me? he thought, almost laughing.

"You're so dedicated to what you're doin'. Ah admire that. Ah'll hafta bake somethin' for you and bring it down to your office."

"I'd like that. I'd like that a lot."

"And do stop ba again when you can. It's so reassurin'."

"I sure will."

When Mathers left Jolene's, he didn't know whether to laugh or cry. He'd gone there more or less on a lark, not really knowing what to expect, and he'd come away thinking he was in love with her. He had no idea whether to chalk up the way she'd acted to Southern belle coquettishness or whether maybe she felt somewhat the same way toward him as he felt toward her. But her husband had only been dead a few weeks. He figured she was grieving and probably desperately lonely and would have been friendly to anyone she trusted who came to see her. And he figured it was probably comforting to her, or anyone in Breda at that point, to have a cop around when there was an insane killer on the loose. He'd noticed that everyone in town was a lot happier to have him around than they'd been before the murders started. It used to be that half the people whose houses he showed up at would seem to resent he was there, like it meant they'd done something wrong. Now they seemed almost overjoyed to see him and didn't mind if he stayed as long as he wanted. For that short time he was there, they thought, for as long as his sheriff's car was in the driveway, they'd be completely safe from the killer.

Maybe Jolene was just like the rest of them.

When Jim went home after talking to Mathers, he only stayed long enough to pack up his clothes and write a letter to Julie. He didn't even say good-by to Bonnie. He figured it would be better if Julie explained his leaving to her. The letter read:

Dear Julie,

I have to get out of town for a while because I'm pretty sure if I stay here my life will be in danger and probably yours will be too. It's probably better if I don't even tell you where I'm going, but I will say I'm going because I think I can solve the murders. I'm going to try to find Moses Kurtz and talk to him. I'll call you soon, but I wanted you to know as soon as you got home what is going on.

I'll call my family later so that you won't get stuck having to try to explain this to everyone. I think Dad's sobered up enough so that he can handle the store for a while. I'm sorry I had to do this, but I really think it's a life or death matter. When I come home, hopefully this nightmare will be over and we can get back to leading something like a normal life.

Just remember I love you more than anything and that nothing really means anything to me without you. I'll miss you every day and (especially) every night I'm gone.

I'll love you always,

Jim

He'd decided to write a letter rather than call her because he didn't want her to try to talk him out of it. He really felt like his life and her life would be in danger if he stayed. Sooner probably rather than later, the killer would make the connection between him and Julie. Also, he'd become obsessed with the idea that if he could find Moses Kurtz, he could solve the murders. He wrote the letter out quickly without really having to think about it much. He'd been composing it in his head while he packed. When he'd finished writing it, though, he read it over a few times, trying to decide if he should add anything more. But he didn't end up changing anything. His bags were already packed. The last thing he did before leaving was to pick up a picture of him and Julie that was on an end table and kiss it.

As Jim drove down to Florida, he thought about Julie a lot, but he thought even more about what strategy he'd use to try to locate Moses Kurtz. All he knew was that he was living in a nursing home somewhere around Ocala. He could go to Ocala and start by looking for his name in the phone book, but he wasn't sure if you lived in a nursing home whether your number would even be in the telephone book. If that didn't work, he'd get a list of nursing homes from the Yellow Pages and call every one on the list. It might turn out to be easier than he thought.

He wondered about the fact that Annie Kurtz Abilene had so readily told him where Moses Kurtz lived. If the Kurtz family had conspired to commit the murders, wouldn't they want to do everything possible to keep his whereabouts a secret? Wouldn't it make more sense to move him and change his name to help make sure no one would look for him and try to talk to him about the curse? The story of the murders in Breda had been published in *Time* and *Newsweek* and gone out on the AP and UPI wires, among other places. Stories about them had probably been on TV stations all over the country. Even in Florida, most people would know about the murders. And who knows what a 95 year old man might say to someone who was investigating the murders? If he hadn't already gone bonkers and could even think straight. On the other hand, Jim still didn't have any idea how many members of the family might be involved. It was most likely just one guy who'd lost his marbles. Even if it was just one guy, though, the others might know or suspect it was him and be trying to cover up for him. At least something like that had to be going on, or Roy Kurtz wouldn't have tried to run him off the road. Could Annie

Abilene have lied to him about where Moses lived to throw him off track?

Jim got so sick of thinking about the murders at times, though, that he tried everything he could to get his mind off them for a while. It was no use thinking about Julie, because then he'd just start worrying about her and would end up thinking about the murders again. He tried concentrating on the scenery: White fences and horse farms and hills in Kentucky, the old wooden unpainted shacks with little porches in Tennessee that looked like something out of Lil' Abner, the red clay fields of Georgia and gleaming skyscrapers of Atlanta. But he could never keep his mind on any of it very long.

He drove straight through, except for a few hours of sleeping at a rest stop in Georgia. By the time he got to Ocala it was night, and he checked in at a cheap motel called Alligators Rest. He spent most of the night worrying about Julie and thinking about finding and talking to Moses Kurtz, so he really didn't get much sleep. But when he woke up in the morning and went outside, it was so pleasant out that he felt refreshed, and for a moment was almost able to forget the horror he'd left behind. The sun was shining, a warm breeze stirred through the palms, and the scent of jasmine was in the air.

This was before Disney World was built in Orlando and the development boom had trickled up to Ocala. It was still more or less a sleepy, peaceful Southern town. Jim walked to the diner across the street from the motel and sat down at a booth. The place was practically empty. A couple of men in suits were talking about business and a fat man in overalls was talking to the owner or manager of the diner about a fishing trip he'd just got back from. The owner looked bored, Jim thought. The waitress soon came over to Jim's booth.

"What can I git for you?" she said.

She was thirtyish and had a nice figure, but her blonde hair was in a bouffant that was years out of style.

"I'd like a cup of coffee and some bacon and eggs," Jim said. "The eggs over easy."

When she brought the coffee she said, "What brings you down this way?"

"What makes you think I'm not from here?" Jim said with a smile.

"Ah can jest tell. Anyway, no one who lives down here is as pale as you are," smiling back.

"I'm down here looking for someone, an old man named Moses Kurtz. The last anyone knew, he was living in an old folks' home around Ocala. You ever hear of him?" doubting there was even a slight chance she would have heard of him.

"No," drawing the word out and looking suspicious, like she was wondering what he was really up to. "But Ocala isn't such a small town that Ah'd know everyone here, not ba a long shot. Especially an old man in an old folks' home. He a relative of yours?"

"No. I'm a private detective. My assignment is to find this guy. Maybe you could tell me where some of these places are," pulling out the nursing home section of the Yellow Pages from his pocket that he'd torn out of the phone book at the Alligators Rest.

She took the page and looked over the addresses and rattled off locations, which Jim tried to remember as much of as he could. He asked her a few questions about the locations and made some notes until he had several of them down pretty well. Most weren't really hard to get to. He was planning to get a map of Ocala anyway, but he was content to talk to the waitress just to pass the time and maybe get some local knowledge that might be of use to him later.

"Why don't you just call them? You could have done that without comin' all the way down here."

"Because, the chances are, where he's staying, they probably don't really want anyone to find him. It's a complicated matter involving an inheritance. And besides, if I'd done that, I wouldn't have had an excuse to come down to Florida."

After Jim had finished his bacon and eggs and Jeannie, the waitress, had wished him good luck, he went out into the warm Florida morning and drove around to some nursing homes. He didn't have much trouble finding them, and the staff he dealt with were mostly friendly and helpful enough. However, none of the homes had a Moses Kurtz living there, and none of the people he talked to—mostly women at reception desks—could remember anyone by that name having stayed in the past. By early afternoon, he was back at the motel watching an old Bowery Boys movie on TV and wondering what to do next. By four o'clock, he was back at the diner, and Jeannie was still on the job.

"Ah'd ask you if you had any luck, but Ah can tell by the way you look you didn't have any," she said when she came over to his table.

"Is it that obvious?" Jim said, smiling. "You're right, I didn't find the guy I'm looking for. And I'm not quite sure where to look next. I was really hoping that the information I had about where he's supposed to be was right. Although he might have been here at one time and been moved."

"Ah know a cop who maght be able to hep you. They have all kinds of ways of findin' people."

"I know all about that. I might take you up on that sooner or later. But I'd rather not get the cops involved in it, because I don't want to explain the story that's behind why I'm looking for him. It's a very delicate situation, if you know what I mean."

"You ain't doin' anything illegal, are you?" with a sidelong look.

"No. And as a matter of fact, if I can find him, it might save some lives."

"Well, well, this story gits more interestin' all the time. An inheritance faght with murders possibly involved."

"It's true. Maybe I'll tell you the whole story some time."

"Ah'd lak to hear it."

She looked into his eyes, thoughtfully, like she was trying to decide something about him.

"Oh, ba the way, would you lak anything to eat?" laughing. "Ah almost forgot."

Jim scanned the menu. "Yeah, bring me a roast beef sandwich with gravy and another cup of coffee."

"Comin' raght up."

Jim had bought a *St. Petersburg Times*, and he read it as he waited for his order. Reading the paper made him wonder how much about the murders had been in the Ocala paper and whether he should tell Jeannie the truth about why he was there.

When Jeannie brought Jim's sandwich, she sat in the chair next to him.

"Ya know, Ah know where there's some old folks homes further out that ain't in the phone book. If you want to, I'm gittin' off at five. I could go with you, and we could check 'em out."

"Sure, why not? It can't hurt. I might even hit the jackpot. And actually, the staff at the nursing homes might be less suspicious if I have a woman with me. I'll just hang out here and read the paper till five."

"All raght. Ah'll jest have to run home first an' change."

An hour later Jim was sitting in the mobile home where Jeannie lived waiting for her to change clothes. The place was a mess, with clothes and magazines and records and dirty dishes scattered all over, and she'd apologized too many times that it was a mess. It was obvious she had more in mind than just being kind to a stranger. She'd already told him that she'd been divorced for a year and wasn't dating anyone right now and was pretty lonely. But there was no way he'd ever be disloyal to Julie, he didn't think. Still, Jeannie was friendly and plenty good looking, and he was glad to have gotten to know someone in Ocala who could help him find Moses Kurtz. He'd just have to tread a very thin line. She came out of her bedroom wearing a blue miniskirt that showed her legs off nicely, and she'd put on a heavy dose of perfume.

"Well, Ah'm ready if you are," she said.

As they drove out of town, the late afternoon sun was filling the clouds with orange and pink behind pastures and palmettos. They had the car windows down, and the scent of orange blossoms was sweet. Jim told Jeannie the whole story of the murders and how because of them, he'd ended up in Ocala. He said he'd made up the story about the inheritance because he had to be real careful who he told the murder story to. His story was punctuated with "oh, mys" and "how awfuls" and "how horribles" from Jeannie. She'd heard about the murders on TV and said everyone in Ocala knew about them.

"Now you know why I'm down here, and why I'm looking for Moses Kurtz," Jim said when he'd finished. "I'm just hoping the old man can tell me something that'll help break the case. I'm just hoping that he'll care about the fact that people are dying for nothing, people who never even knew who Obadiah Kurtz was, and that he'll understand that Obadiah's death can never be avenged by killing innocent people. That he won't want the killings hanging over his head when he dies and that he'll tell me who in his family could possibly be committing them."

Jim almost started crying as the tragedy of the killings hit him full force again, and as he realized the probable futility of what he was trying to do. Jeannie put her hand on his arm.

"This has got to be the worst thing Ah've ever heard of," she said. "Ah just wish there was more Ah could do to hep."

"You've done plenty already. It's nice to have somebody to talk to around here and knows the area."

To a few retirement homes they went and came up with nothing. Jim was about to tell Jeannie he was ready to quit looking. The whole idea of what he was doing was getting to seem more and more a waste of time. It seemed likely that Annie Kurtz Abilene had just flat out lied to him or didn't really know anymore where Moses Kurtz lived. Maybe Moses Kurtz was dead. But Jim kept on going.

"That's the place Ah was talkin' about," Jeannie said, pointing to what looked like a plantation house up ahead. The place was well lit, with tall white pillars.

"May I help you?" the receptionist said when Jim and Jeannie went inside.

"We're here to visit Mr. Moses Kurtz," Jim said.

"We don't have anyone living here by that name. I'm sorry," she said.

"Do you remember anyone ever living here by that name?"

This was in the days before privacy laws were around, and people would actually answer questions like that.

She laughed. "Not in the last month. That's all I've been here. Maybe Mr. Cowley would remember." She picked up the phone to page him.

In a moment, a tall, bald, imposing man came into the reception hall.

"This man's looking for a Moses Kurtz, who he thinks may have lived here once. You ever hear of him?"

"I'm afraid no one with that name has ever lived here. I've been here since the Shady Palms opened, and I'm sure I'd remember a name like that."

He looked right into Jim's eyes with a piercing gaze.

"I guess we might as well leave then and try someplace else," Jim said.

"Sorry we couldn't be of help."

As they were driving away, Jim said, "There was something about that guy. I don't believe him. I think he really knows who Moses Kurtz is."

"The way he looked at me gave me the chills," Jeannie said. "But Ah don' know. He seemed lak the kind of guy who'd lie to you the same way he'd tell you the truth."

"Or maybe I'm just kidding myself," with a laugh edged with bitterness. "Maybe I'm getting like the people back in Breda who're so busted up by the killings that they don't trust anyone anymore and who have delusions about their neighbors plotting to kill them."

"Ah sure hope not. You trust me, don't ya?"

He looked over at her and smiled.

"I'm not even sure I trust myself."

"The next place's about five miles further on, called Southern Hills."

"I don't even want to go there. I want to find out more about the Shady Palms, and if I'm wrong, I might just give up looking for the guy. I'm not going to live long enough to check out every old folks' home in Florida, and even if I could, I might not find him."

When they got back to Ocala, Jim knew he should just drop Jeannie off at her mobile home and go back to his motel, but he was lonely, and she really wanted him to stick around. She turned on *The Mary Tyler Moore Show*, and they sat on her wornout sofa. As they watched the show, Jeannie jabbered on and on about work and her family and her ex-husband—whom she despised—but Jim didn't say much at all. He more or less kept his eyes glued to the set, even though Jeannie kept looking over at him. He had a lot on his mind, and he didn't want to let happen what he figured was on her mind. He wondered how soon he could leave without seeming rude.

"Can Ah fix you somethin' to eat?"

"No, I'm not hungry. I wouldn't mind another beer, though."

When she came back with the beer, she sat close to him and put her hand on his leg.

"It musta been maghty lonely comin' down here ba yourself," she said, rubbing his leg.

"I had too much on my mind to get lonely," Jim said.

He looked into Jeannie's eyes, and he knew that he had to do something, that he couldn't just let things slide anymore, because she wasn't going to let them. She brought her other hand up to his neck and caressed it.

"I shouldn't be doing this, you know," he said.

"You ain't doin' nothing yet."

He let her pull his head down, and they put their arms around each other and kissed, and it was so sweet, especially because he'd been so lonely and down since he'd left Julie, that he didn't know if he'd be able to stop himself now. They kissed for a long time and Jeannie took one of Jim's hands and rubbed it softly against her chest. But Jim broke off the kiss.

"I've gotta go." He expected her to say something, but she just stared at him, while an Alka-Seltzer commercial played in the background. "I'd better go because I'm engaged to someone back home, and this isn't fair to her, and it isn't fair to you."

She pulled away from him.

"Git the hell out of here then! Why in the hell did you even let it go this far?"

"Because I was lonely as hell, and you didn't exactly discourage me."

"Well, I'm discouraging you now," pushing him away. "Just get out of here!"

Jim thought she looked like she was about to cry. He didn't know what to think. It seemed like such an overreaction to what had happened. Apparently, he thought, she was a lot lonelier and was counting on a lot more than he'd imagined.

Chapter 9

Only a few people lived in Breda Mathers could trust who were old enough and had lived in town long enough to remember much about the curse. And after he'd talked to them about it, he didn't come away feeling he knew any more about it than Jim did. The old timers would nod their head when he asked them about it, and tell him what they could remember, but none of it really meant anything. Part of it was that most of them had been so beaten down mentally by the infirmity of age or by fear of the murders, that they didn't seem to be as much in touch with reality as a normal person would. Most of them didn't really look at Mathers—they just kind of gazed off into the distance and muttered short sentences or phrases that didn't provide much information. He got the feeling they didn't want to talk about the curse or about anything that had to do with the murders, that they just wanted Mathers to go away. Virtually that they'd given up on life. Some of them he thought acted like they were waiting fatalistically for the murderer to kill them and didn't care much about anything anymore. None of them said they'd thought about a connection between the murders and the curse. It was too long ago.

Mathers didn't learn much more when he talked to a few people over in Morrisey about the Kurtzes, either. Everybody thought they were strange birds. When Mathers talked to Harvey King, the county sheriff, he found out Roy Kurtz had once been a deputy with the department but had been fired for mistreating suspects and prisoners. One of the suspects, a certain Jeffrey Greenberg who turned out to be innocent, had sued the department over an incident involving Kurtz, and the county had lost a bundle.

Mathers went to visit Roy Kurtz at his house on the outskirts of Morrisey. Though the house was small and not kept up well, it had curlicue moldings under the edge of the roof and fancy shutters that gave it a certain quaintness. It could have been a charming little house if someone had put some work into it. But weeds had taken over the lawn, and paint was peeling off the house. One of the shutters looked like it was about to fall off.

Kurtz was hostile from the moment he answered the door.

"What do you want?" he said.

"I'm Sheriff Bill Mathers of Van Dyke County," Mathers said, taking out his badge and showing it to Kurtz. "I've got some questions I'd like to ask you."

"Out of your jurisdiction, aren't you?"

"I met with Harvey King before I came over and got his permission. He said you used to work for the department."

"Yeah. The asshole fired me. He didn't like the way I handled prisoners. He thought we were running a hotel or something."

"A man from Breda almost got run off the road after he left the Black Maria tavern last Thursday afternoon to drive home. He believes you were the one who did it."

"I don't know anything about it, Mathers. I never left the bar."

"I'll bet you wouldn't know anything about any of the murders over in Breda, either, would you?"

"Only what I read in the paper about how you've botched the case."

"I must have missed that article. I understand you Kurtzes don't like Breda very much."

"We haven't shed any tears over what's happened over there. But we didn't have anything to do with any of the killings. It just shows how desperate you are that you'd even think we do, just because of what a bunch of old ladies say about a curse my great-grandfather supposedly put on Breda a hundred years ago. Don't you think it's kind of late for us to be getting our revenge? Do you think any of us even give a fuck any more since none of us ever even knew him?"

"Your grandfather Moses knew him."

Roy Kurtz was silent a moment before he replied. There was a certain movement in his eyes such that Mathers knew Kurtz was surprised he knew about Moses.

"Is that what you think? That a 95 year old man who lives in Florida who can't even walk anymore killed all those people? Do you think he's a Led Zeppelin fan, too? If that's the best theory you can come up with, if I were you, I'd turn in my badge and let someone smarter take over the case. My professional judgment is you're in over your head."

"You're not in the profession anymore, remember? You got kicked out."

"I wanted to leave anyway. King's a jerk."

It was obvious to Mathers from the start that Kurtz wasn't going to tell him anything of value. But he wanted to see what he was like, size him up a little. There was no reason to stay any longer.

"I've got to go now," he said. "There're some other people I need to talk to."

"Why don't you go down to Florida and talk to Moses and waste more of your department's money? Maybe the two of you can go to a Led Zeppelin concert together. I'll bet Moses killed all these people. He can really get around in that wheelchair of his."

"Thanks for your help," Mathers said sarcastically as he started to walk away. "It's guys like you that make this job fun."

"Any time," Kurtz said. "I'm always happy to help you guardians of public safety."

Mathers thought Kurtz seemed like an anti-social character, and obviously he had a violent side. Yet somehow, he couldn't imagine him committing the murders, and he doubted he knew anything about them. Whatever else Roy Kurtz was, he didn't seem to Mathers like a psychopath, and Mathers believed that only a psychopath could have carried out the Breda killings. It just seemed to him like Roy Kurtz enjoyed giving him a hard time and might even want him to consider him a suspect to make his job harder and make the investigation more confusing. He left as puzzled as when he'd started.

Mathers decided not to wait any longer to tell Quentin and Pursley about the curse theory, since he wasn't getting anywhere with it himself. He drove to Grand Rapids to see them right after he talked to Roy Kurtz.

"I've got another theory for you," Mathers said. They were sitting in Pursley's office. Pursley was behind his desk, Mathers was sitting in a chair in front of the desk, and Quentin was standing at the doorway, leaning against it.

"Oh, yeah?" Pursley said, gruffly. "Now what?"

Mathers waited a moment before he spoke. Suddenly the theory seemed ridiculous.

"There was a curse put on Breda in 1889 by a man named Obadiah Kurtz. He was hanged allegedly for killing his wife, but apparently it was a bum rap. She really died of natural causes. The real reason he was killed was that he was different, because the Dutch Reformed ministers were afraid of him or really thought he was an agent of Satan. The story goes that Obadiah put a curse on Breda just before he was hanged. He said one of his sons or the sons of his sons would avenge his death. All the victims of the Breda Killer so far are descendants of the men responsible for Obadiah's hanging except Evelyn Rijssen. And maybe even she fits in somewhere. Maybe someone else was involved in the hanging who I don't know about yet. I know it sounds crazy, and you can ignore it if you want to. I just thought I'd let you know."

Normally, Mathers thought, Quentin and Pursley would have just laughed a story like that off. They probably would have interrupted him before he even finished. But he'd finished the story, and still they hadn't said anything. They were interested but didn't want to admit it, Mathers thought. The pressure to solve this case was enormous, and it was getting to them.

"How did you find that out?" Pursley said.

"A man from Breda named Jim Leiden researched the story from old newspaper stories and talking to old timers in Breda and from county birth records. He's in Florida right now trying to track down Moses Kurtz, Obadiah's son. He's about 95 years old and supposedly is living in a nursing home around Ocala, Florida."

Quentin scoffed.

"He's probably working on a tan and chasing bikinis."

"After Leiden told me the story, I did a little investigating myself. I've got a list of potential victims based on the family trees that Leiden constructed from the birth records. Here's a copy of it if you want to take a look at it."

He took the Xerox copy of the Death List from his pocket and handed it to Pursley, who looked it over carefully.

"This doesn't mean anything," Pursley said. "After this much time, half the people in Breda could be related in one way or the other to the men who hanged this Obadiah Kurtz. And Evelyn Rijssen's not on it anyway, just like you said."

"I didn't say I believed the theory," Mathers said. "I just thought I'd tell you about it. Everybody seems to be out of good ideas."

"Well, I don't think it means a damn thing," Pursley said. But he kept the list and put it in his pocket.

"That's up to you. I just thought I'd let you experts evaluate it. I'm not supposed to be able to figure stuff like this out, remember?" sarcastically but smiling a little.

"We'll let you know what we come up with," Quentin said, with heavy irony.

Mathers knew it didn't mean anything that Quentin and Pursley acted like they didn't believe the theory. They would have acted the same way whether they believed it or not. Of course, if there was anything to it, they'd try to take all the credit in the end. He thought it would be interesting to see if they did any investigating into it.

Kurtz was becoming more and more obsessed with the matter of Jim Leiden. He was the one person who could mess everything up, the one fly in the ointment. Kurtz had found out Jim had left for Florida. Was he searching for Moses? If he found him, who knows but what the senile old man might not tell him something? Kurtz had foolishly told Moses what he was going to do. Not told him in so many words that he was going to destroy Breda, or murder anyone for that matter. Just that he was going to get even with the town for the horrible insult and humiliation and death that had been brought upon the Kurtz family. He wanted him to have the satisfaction of knowing that finally the family was going to be avenged for the crime that had taken away the old man's father when Moses was only a boy and had crippled and disgraced his life. Kurtz remembered the smile on Moses' face when he'd told him. Wasn't he happy, knowing he would go to his grave knowing Breda had finally been made to pay? That he wouldn't have to die with the anguish of his father's murder still gnawing away at him?

But who could predict what the old man might do if presented with the facts of the murders? Who's to say whether he might not soften up and tell Leiden that he was probably behind them? Even though he'd paid the manager of the Shady Palms, where Moses had lived for ten years, good money not to tell anyone he'd lived there, there was no guarantee that Leiden wouldn't be persistent enough—or get dumb lucky—and find where Kurtz had moved him. The thing had worked perfectly so far. Since no one in the Kurtz family came to see Moses anymore, and since Moses was too frail and too out of it to call or write anyone, everyone in the Kurtz family would think Moses was still at the Shady Palms. He thought again how smart he'd been to move Moses—just as an extra precaution. Otherwise, who knows? Maybe Leiden would already have found him.

Kurtz had to kill Jim Leiden or at least get him out of Florida. Killing him would be especially hard because he'd actually have to go down to Florida and hope that Leiden didn't leave before he got down there. And if Leiden saw him down there before Kurtz could kill him, and recognized him because he'd seen him around Breda, the whole game would be up. Leiden would probably put two and two together instantly and realize there was only one reason someone else from around Breda would be in Ocala, Florida, at the same time he was. Nope, that was just too risky. Then he laughed as he thought of a sure way to bring Leiden back from Florida fast: Kill Julie Veere. His chair creaked on the wooden floor as counterpoint to his laughter, and as he looked out, he saw the moon faintly through tattered clouds. The house was so silent and dreary that being there alone on a night like that would have given almost anyone else the creeps. But it was the setting that Kurtz liked the most: Complete solitude to consider the rage and sense of injustice he felt about the hanging of his great grandfather, work out his Master Plan, and savor the suffering and anguish he'd brought to Breda.

His next goal was clear: He must kill Julie Veere. Now there was just the matter of method. It wouldn't be any cinch because she lived in the center of town around a lot of other houses and was sure to be on her guard constantly, but he was sure he'd think of something. He always did.

Jim couldn't ever remember feeling more lonely and depressed than he did after he left Jeannie's mobile home. He felt like he was the only person on earth, and the other people he saw were only shades or cartoon characters that he couldn't communicate with. He tried calling Julie, but there was no answer. He wondered where she could be that late and if she was OK. The only thing that kept him from being completely overwhelmed with melancholy was the need to plan a strategy to investigate the Shady Palms, to see if there was anything to his hunch that Moses Kurtz really had lived there. The best idea seemed to be to drive out there in the morning before it got too hot but after the residents would be done with breakfast, at a time when a lot of the them would be outside and the manager would probably be inside. Then to look for the people who looked the most coherent and talk to as many of them as he could before he aroused any suspicion. The ideal thing would be to stay there just a few minutes. Even if he did find out Moses Kurtz had lived there, it could all be wasted if the manager spotted him and told the Kurtz family.

Jim arrived at the Shady Palms about 10 o'clock the next morning. He drove past it first to check it out, and the setting seemed ideal. Ten or twelve elderly people were out sitting on the lawn, and the manager was nowhere to be seen. The only person who looked like a staff member was a guy dressed in white who was serving lemonade to a couple of white haired women sitting at a table. Only a few cars were in the parking lot. Jim parked in the back of the lot next to the car that was farthest from the entrance to the Shady Rest. The scent of orange blossoms perfumed the air deliciously. In a moment, he was talking to the two old women who he'd seen being served drinks.

"Good morning, ladies," Jim said, smiling. "Could you tell me if a man named Moses Kurtz ever lived here?"

The two women looked at each other like they were both trying to remember.

"I don't believe I've met anyone by that name here," one of them said.

"I haven't either," the other said. "But we've only been here a few months. Ask Mr. Coolidge," pointing to a man in a wheel chair. "To hear him talk you'd think he was born here and never left," laughing.

"Thanks, I'll do that," Jim said.

Jim walked over to the man and asked him if he knew Moses Kurtz.

"Sure, he lived here for ten years," Mr. Coolidge said. "Then one night his grandson or somebody came and took him away, and I never heard nothin' about him again. I thought it was strange. He never said nothin' about goin' nowhere and then poof, he was gone," hitting his palms together.

Though Mr. Coolidge looked about as old as anyone Jim had ever seen, crouched in his wheelchair with just a few wisps of white hair left on his head, Jim thought his mind seemed crystal clear. He had no reason to doubt what he said. He didn't get any more time to discuss it, though, because Mr. Cowley, the manager of the Shady Palms, and two burly men dressed in white came up to him. One of them grabbed Jim from the back and held him by the arms.

"What in the hell are you doing back here?" Cowley said.

"I came to visit an old friend of mine," Jim said. "We graduated from high school together."

"Very funny. Do you want to get the hell out of here right now, or do you need a little persuasion first?"

"It won't do you any good now. This gentleman has already told me that Moses Kurtz lived here for ten years. You must have a pretty rotten memory."

Cowley didn't reply at first, like he was thinking about what the implications of Jim knowing Moses Kurtz had lived there might be.

"Why the hell do you want to know about an old man like that so bad for? And don't hand me that bullshit you told me last night."

"It just so happens that a relative of his may have committed four murders in Breda, Michigan. You may have heard about the Breda Killer."

"Yeah, I've heard about him. But I think you're lying. What the hell could a 95 year old man possibly know about a bunch of murders?"

"He might know plenty, and he might know nothing. That's what I'm trying to find out. How in the hell much did the Kurtz family pay you to lie for them?"

"It's none of your goddamn business whether they paid me anything. I think you're a lying son-of-a-bitch, and I still say that nobody named Moses Kurtz ever lived here. This old man's senile. He doesn't even know who lived here yesterday, much less ten years ago."

"He's got more brains than you do, as far as I can tell. I'll bet he's smart enough not to let anyone pay him to lie for him, when he could end up in prison for it."

"I've listened to enough of your shit. If you're not out of here in one minute, I'll have these guys teach you a lesson you'll never forget," looking at his watch and motioning to the guy who was holding Jim to let him go. "And don't waste your time going to the police. Around here they're all good friends of mine."

"You'd better have lots of friends in the FBI, too," Jim said as he walked away. "I'm sure they'll be very interested in this development."

"They'll never listen to a lying sack of shit like you," Cowley said.

As Jim was walking away, he noticed the old folks looking at him warily, as if they didn't want Cowley to notice they'd been watching. He wondered what kind of hold Cowley had over them and figured it was pretty strong. No doubt they were all afraid of him. He got in his car and drove away but looked in his rearview mirror often to see if anyone tried to follow him. No one seemed to, although after a while he saw a blue Chevy 50 yards or so behind him and wondered about it.

He had a hell of a lot to think about on the ride back to his motel. He was excited about finding out Moses Kurtz had lived at the Shady Palms but wondered how much it really meant. Even if he could get the police to question Cowley, Jim was sure he would just deny everything. And even if the police could get Cowley to admit that Moses Kurtz had lived at the Shady Palms, there was a fairly good chance he didn't know where Moses had been taken to. Or that he'd known the true identity of whoever had paid him to keep quiet about Moses Kurtz. He doubted that Cowley had known anything about the connection to the murders before Jim had told him. He probably just thought the whole thing had to do with some kind of family squabble.

Of two things, though, Jim was sure. He should let Bill Mathers know right away what he'd discovered, and he should get out of Ocala before Cowley and his thugs had a chance to find out where he was staying. It wasn't much fun speculating about what Cowley might do if he did find him. Jim had no idea what kind of arrangements he had with the Kurtz family. Cowley might even try to kill him. Jim knew the only thing that had saved his skin at the retirement home was that there were about twenty potential witnesses staring right at him and Cowley, and no matter how afraid they were of him, he couldn't count on getting all of them to lie for him. Jim wasn't sure about where he should go next. Should he stay in Florida and somehow try to ferret out where Moses Kurtz? Should he go back to Breda? He missed Julie terribly and worried about her constantly. But he still was inclined to think she might be safer without him there, since he was pretty sure the Kurtz family was after him.

As soon as Jim got back to the Alligators Rest, he called Bill Mathers. There was no phone in his room, so he called him from the pay phone outside the motel.

"Bill, I think I've come across something that could be a major break in the case," Jim said.

"Oh, yeah?" Mathers said.

"I found out that Moses Kurtz was living in Florida, in a retirement home called the Shady Palms, near Ocala, until fairly recently. Then he was mysteriously moved out one night by someone who paid the manager, a guy named John Cowley, to pretend he'd never lived there. The only thing that'll make all that make any sense is that he knows something about the murders."

"How in the hell did you find all that out?"

"A little bit of luck and a hell of a lot of driving around Ocala checking out retirement homes and nursing homes. But I don't think there's much else I can do. Wherever they've taken Moses Kurtz, he's probably registered under a phony name if he's registered at a home at all. He may not even be in Florida anymore."

"It's probably more likely that he isn't."

"If this is ever going to get anywhere, the police have to get involved, somebody who can convince Cowley that it's in his best interest to talk or get some kind of bulletin put out to try to locate Moses Kurtz."

"I'll talk to the other investigators and see what I can come up with. Then I'll come down there to see if I can find him myself."

"OK. Do your best. I'm planning on getting out of here before the goons who work for Cowley can find me. There's no telling what they might do. And there's no telling what kind of deal Cowley has with the Kurtzes, or how deeply involved he is with the whole scheme."

"You coming back here?"

"I don't think so. I'd rather wait until you get down here, and we can look for Moses Kurtz together. But I really want to come back, too."

"Be careful. If you don't come right back, call my office tomorrow so I'll know where you are."

"I sure will."

When Mathers hung up, he sat at his desk for a long time thinking about what Jim had told him. He was convinced there really was something to Jim's theory, but there were still a lot of question marks in his mind about it and some things about it that didn't totally make sense. Like even if someone in the Kurtz family had committed the murders, why would a 95 year old man get involved with it or been told anything about it? He couldn't possibly have been any help in carrying them out. He asked himself the questions he knew the state police detectives and the investigators from the attorney general's office would ask and imagined how they would react. Even with the new twist that Jim had added to the Kurtz theory, it still sounded pretty farfetched. But it was about all Mathers thought about the rest of the day. Then that night something really bizarre happened. Mathers was sleeping when the phone rang and was groggy and wondered how long it had been ringing when he picked it up.

"Oh, Bill, please come over as quickly as you can," Jolene said, practically screaming. "Ah think someone's tryin' to break into ma house."

"Take your gun and stand in the middle of your living room facing where you think the noise is coming from. I'll be right over."

Jumping out of bed, he put some clothes on and grabbed his police pistol and ran outside to his squad car. He wondered if he should radio other police to meet him at Jolene's, but he wanted to be her hero and be with her alone to rescue her. If he'd thought about it, he'd have realized how selfish that was and how it might even risk her life. But he didn't have time to think about it. All he had time to think about was how he'd handle the situation when he got to Jolene's house. At least before the Breda Killer, most of this type of "emergency" turned out to be false alarms anyway.

He was in her driveway less than 15 minutes after she called. The first thing he did was to run around the house, with his gun drawn, to see if anyone was trying to break in. Then he went to the front door and rang the doorbell as he shouted, "It's me, Jolene."

She opened the door, dressed in a short robe and crying.

"What's happened since you called?" Mathers said.

"Nothin'. Ah didn't hear anything more."

"The first thing I'd better do is check out the house. While I'm doing that, stay in the center of the living room with your gun in your hand just like I told you on the phone."

Mathers went through every room in the house, checking every place a person could hide, but didn't find anything or hear anything. On the contrary, the house was eerily quiet. He made sure the outside doors were locked. Then he went back to the living room.

"Whoever it was, they're gone now," feeling almost certain that whatever she'd heard had been all in her mind. He'd used the same words dozens of other times since the murders had started, when he'd been called in the middle of the night by frantic people who heard murderers everywhere. He never suggested to anyone that what they'd heard might just be a figment of their imagination, even though he figured most of them knew that's what he was thinking. But this time was different. Jolene was still standing in the middle of the room with the gun in her hand, and she was shaking.

"Let me take that," Mathers said, taking the gun from her hand and setting it on an end table. "There's nothing to worry about now."

They looked into each other's eyes, Jolene's glassy with tears, and Mathers was stunned once again by their beauty and by his extraordinary attraction to her.

"Ah can't take it anymore, Bill. Ah've got to get out of here," and she put her arms around Mathers, and he put his around her, and they held each other tightly.

When she looked up at him they kissed, and he felt her tremendous passion surging through him, like she'd kept it bottled up ever since her husband had died and probably a long time before that and was letting it all spill out at once.

For a long time, they didn't even speak, just broke off kissing occasionally to look at each other and smile, and even when they went to Jolene's bed they didn't speak, just held hands as they walked there, like they could read each other's minds. It was like they were both exhausted from speaking, like all the words they had wasted talking and worrying about the murders had worn them out, and they felt tremendous relief at not having to say anything for a while.

When they had taken their clothes off and put their arms around each other under the covers, Jolene moaned softly and laughed the tiniest laugh. Mathers felt a passion and a love unlike any he'd ever felt before or even knew existed. Certainly it was unlike anything he'd ever known in his marriage. They made love for a long time before saying anything. Then they held each other close and looked into each other's eyes, with just the light from the hallway shining in dimly.

"You can't imagine how lonely Ah've been," Jolene said. "Ah thought Ah was gonna die."

Mathers wondered whether she really cared about him or whether she'd gotten so lonely she couldn't stand it anymore, and he just happened to be there at the right time. But right now, he wasn't going to let it worry him.

"I think everyone in Breda has been, even people who live in a house full of people. The murders have made everyone withdraw into their own little world."

That was the kind of cheap philosophizing Mathers normally laughed at, but somehow now it seemed all right.

"Ah've been wanting this to happen for a long time, but Ah didn't know how you felt and at first Ah was worried about the scandal it would cause. But now scandals don't seem to matter so much."

"I've been wanting it to happen, too, but I never thought in a million years that it would."

"Why?" smiling. "Did Ah just seem too hagh and maghty to you?"

"Something like that. As religious as you are, I thought it would be at least a year before you'd go out with anyone, and I didn't think you'd ever be interested in a cop."

"It sounds lak you've been thinkin' about me quite a bit," laughing and kissing Mathers on the lips.

"Maybe I have. Maybe I have a lot more than I had any business to."

"Well, Ah've thought about you, too. Ah even wished you could stay the night Larry was found, and you were so sweet to me. Not to sleep with me, but just to keep me company. But that made me feel so guilty."

Mathers pulled Jolene closer and they kissed some more.

"Don't you just wish we could stay lak this forever, and forget all the sad and tragic things in the world?" Jolene said.

"I just wish it was that easy," Mathers said, and they made love again.

They spent the rest of the night making love and cuddling and talking and didn't fall asleep until streaks of pale sunlight began filtering into the room.

Chapter 10

Jim planned to leave Ocala the day he found out Moses Kurtz had lived at the Shady Rest, but he didn't rush because he didn't figure there was any way Cowley could find out where he was that fast. After all, Cowley could have no idea where he was staying. For all he knew, Jim could have driven in from Georgia or Miami, or any place in between, and left the same day.

So it was about five o'clock before Jim actually checked out of the Alligators Rest and left Ocala. He hadn't quite decided yet where he was going. More than anything he wanted to see Julie again, but he was still afraid he might jeopardize her life if he went back to Breda. And he wanted to stay in Florida if Mathers was going to get a search effort going for Moses Kurtz. He'd virtually become obsessed with seeing the old man and talking to him. But he decided he'd better get at least an hour's drive away from Ocala to stay out of harm's way.

On back roads, Jim drove north for about an hour and ended up stopping at the Blue Bell Diner in a little town called Palmetto Grove. It was a quiet little town, more like the Florida of fifty years ago than the glitzy Miami kind of Florida most people from the north thought of when they thought of the state back then. The waitress at the Bluebird was friendly, and Jim felt relaxed as he read the *St. Petersburg Times* and drank coffee with the cheeseburger and apple pie he'd ordered. He ignored the stories about Vietnam and Nixon and mostly just read the sports section. The scent of jasmine coming through the open windows he thought was lovely, and he was somewhat able to get his mind off his troubles for a while.

The peaceful scene continued when Jim left the Bluebird and started driving again. Palm fronds waved in the breeze beneath blue sky and fluffy white clouds. He drove by the quaint old buildings of the little town out to the cattle farms north of it. It was near sunset. He hadn't driven more than a few miles, however, before his car started to drag like the tires didn't have enough air in them. Within another mile, the tires didn't have any air in them at all, and the car virtually came to a halt. Jim got out of his car and saw that all four of the tires were flat, and also that a blue Chevy just like the one that he'd seen when he'd left the Shady Palms was pulling up behind him. It didn't take a genius to figure out what had happened. Jim left his car and began running across a cattle field, wondering if whoever was in the Chevy would shoot at him. He was glad the cattle didn't chase him, that they just looked at him strangely, and he tried to come up with a strategy. There were no houses within sight. The pasture seemed to go on forever. Jim thought his only hope of losing the two guys—who were already out of their car and running after him—was to run into a palm glade on the opposite side of the pasture. That it was big enough to get lost in, or that there'd be a house on the other side of it, he'd just have to hope.

He was starting to run out of breath, and when he
looked behind him, the two guys were running after him
and seemed to be gaining on him. The glade was still
quite a ways away. The odor of the cattle manure—which
he also occasionally stepped in—didn't make breathing
any easier. He wondered if the guys running after him
were hurting as much as he was, and how long they'd keep
running if they didn't catch him. He'd been a track star at
Breda High School, and he figured they'd have to be really
fast to catch him. Then he was too tired even to think
anymore. Finally, he got into the sawgrass that led up to the
glade. It was so tall Jim practically had to come to a
stop, and it didn't get much shorter—just wetter—when he
got to the cabbage palms. He pushed ahead with every
ounce of strength he had left, constantly changing
direction in hope of losing the guys who were after him. His
hands were covered with mud from when he'd fallen in the
swampy ground and his shoes were covered with mud and
soaked through, and mosquitoes were biting him. He got
mud on his face when he wiped the mosquitoes off, and it
mixed with the sweat that covered his face and made a weird
odor. Because it slowed him down, he'd stopped looking
behind him, but he thought he could hear the guys getting
closer. It was almost like they knew exactly where he was
going. Finally, when Jim reached the other side of the glade,
which opened up to another pasture filled with cattle and
cattle egrets that stretched to the horizon, he felt a hand on
his shoulder and knew he was doomed. A moment later,
he felt a knee in his ass and he fell on his face to the
ground. The two guys were standing over him, breathing
heavily, dressed in dark pants and white short sleeved

shirts that were as muddy and messed up as Jim's clothes. They were the same two guys who John Cowley had threatened him with at the Shady Palms.

"Too bad you're such a nosy little boy," one of them said. "You've caused a lot of trouble."

He had a pistol in his hand and was pointing it at Jim.

"It won't do you any good to kill me," Jim said, barely able to get the words out because he was breathing so hard.

"We'll decide whether it'll do any good or not," the same guy said. "We don't need your help."

"The state police in Michigan and the FBI and everybody else already know all about Cowley and the Shady Palms, and they'll be down here tomorrow, if not today, to check it out."

"Well, they won't find us, will they?" looking over at his buddy, who nodded but didn't seem inclined to talk much. "We're way up here teaching someone a lesson," kicking Jim.

Jim felt pain shoot through his side. He knew that anything he said would probably be wasted, that they had a perfect opportunity to kill him and would probably take advantage of it. He thought of Julie, how much he loved her, and how the thought of never seeing her again, never hearing her voice again, was almost worse than death itself.

"Whatever they're paying you, it isn't worth it," he said. "Cowley's ass is grass and yours are, too, if you stick with him. No amount of money he can pay you will do you any good if you get sent to the electric chair."

He stood up.

"I'm sick of discussing it, boy. I didn't come here to get into a debate. If we ever see you in Florida again or if you say anything about what you've seen down here, we'll kill you."

He nodded to the other guy, who proceeded to hit Jim in the face and knock him to the ground again. His head reeled as if it had been torn from his body. He was nearly knocked out. They kicked him all over and hit him on the head with their guns. He cried out in pain with every blow but didn't have enough strength left to even try to crawl away. He looked up into the darkening sky and the palms and palmettos, and they started to blur. Everything turned black, and then finally there was nothing.

Kurtz did virtually nothing for days but think and plan about how he could kill Julie Veere. He spent as much time as he could watching her house and her, trying to put together the pattern of her life. For a long time, he felt a maddening anger because there didn't seem to be any chink in her routine that would make it possible to pull off a foolproof murder. It was clear to him that she'd made an all out effort to protect herself. Every morning she carpooled to work in Grand Rapids with Gina Matthews, who lived only three doors down, so she was never alone on the way to work. Kurtz had pondered for a time the idea of waylaying the car on their way to work and killing them both. He was thrilled with how a double murder would add a new twist of terror to his rampage. But there didn't seem to be any way to pull it off. The road from Breda to Grand Rapids was heavily traveled during the times Julie and Gina drove to and from work. It wasn't possible he could run them off the road anywhere along the route and not have people see it.

The location of Julie's house near the center of town, combined with the fact the roads and streets all over Breda were patrolled day and night now by the state police and county sheriff's deputies, made an easy murder at her house impossible, too. She made few trips outside of her house anymore, either, and when she did, it wasn't in any predictable manner. She had spent most of her free time since Jim left keeping her mother company or reading or watching TV. The neighborhood patrols that had been set up all over Breda because of the murders could bring out a small army of people with guns at the slightest alarm or sign of trouble. To top it off, both she and her neighbors now had lights installed all around their houses that burned through the night, and her house, and it seemed like every other house around it, had a noisy and vicious dog. And if that weren't enough, Julie carried a small pistol with her now everywhere she went. For the longest time, the whole thing drove Kurtz to no end of frustration, so that sometimes he would cry out as he sat in his chair at his house looking out over the empty night landscape.

He was becoming more and more obsessed with the idea of murdering Julie. It would be a perfect piece in his Master Plan if he could pull it off. She was so beautiful and young, and everyone in town loved her, and best of all, she was the woman Jim Leiden loved. If I could kill her, Kurtz thought, Leiden would want to come back here so fast he'd wish he were an astronaut. He'd be crushed, a broken man. He wouldn't care about the murders anymore. Everything he lived for would be gone, and he'd probably slink out of town never to be heard from again—and Kurtz would be that much closer to his final triumph. It would be so much sweeter than killing Mabel Valden. He'd gotten cold comfort from that. At least he'd made the point there was no escape from him. But only a murder much more daring and destructive could excite him now.

When Kurtz finally did come up with his plan to kill Julie, it so pleased him that he cried out with joy in much the same way as he had in frustration before. He didn't know why he hadn't thought of it before. It was so simple and would be so easy. Of course, he should have realized that he'd never be able to kill Julie in any ordinary way. Too many things were in place now to prevent that. Kurtz's idea was a different angle, a different approach than he'd used before, that would leave the police and the terrified citizenry of Breda more baffled than ever. What he'd do is concoct a perfect disguise and get Julie to let him in the house voluntarily, then pull off the murder. The disguise would be so perfect that even if everyone in town saw him, they'd have no idea who he really was.

Once Kurtz had the concept of the murder down, he was able to relish the rest of the planning, like deciding what sort of disguise he would use and the method of the actual killing. The two disguises that immediately came into his mind were clergyman and policeman. At this point in Breda, those were probably the only two kinds of strangers that anyone in Breda was likely to let into their house, especially at night. And even though

Kurtz's plan was to use a disguise, he felt it was imperative the murder be carried out at night. The only time Julie was home during the week was at night, and he didn't want to take a chance on trying to pull off the murder on a weekend. There were too many unpredictable elements at work on weekends, and too many people were out coming and going. Kurtz quickly rejected the idea of policeman. First of all, he was pretty sure that everyone in Breda knew all the cops in the area, especially since the murders, and the cops sure all knew one another. But the biggest problem with impersonating a cop is it would leave him no chance to disguise his face. Everybody knows that cops don't wear beards, he thought. And there were other problems, too, like coming up with a badge and ID. No, that just wouldn't do. Clergyman, on the other hand, would be easy. There were lots of clergymen in the world, so he figured there must be a lot of places that sell clergymen's shirts. To that he'd add a beard. He wasn't so well known around town that people would recognize him with a beard—especially if he wore a hat. He wasn't sure exactly what he'd have to do to get a fake beard, but they did it on TV all the time, so he figured there must be a way. He'd find out. With that, he didn't think there was any chance Julie would recognize him. He hadn't had any real contact with her anyway.

There were some problems. It was chancy as far as whether Julie would let him in the house. The last thing a lot of people want to see at their door at night is some reverend who wants to hit them up for cash or try to convert them. And even though Julie was especially kind and polite, there was no guarantee she'd let him in if he were dressed up like a clergyman. But he didn't need for her to let him in. All she had to do was open the door one little crack and he'd force his way in.

He was tremendously pleased with himself. With all the murders he'd committed, this was the time he enjoyed the most, when he had a perfect murder plan in place and all that remained was to carry it out. It was at these moments, too, that his feelings of vengeance were most acute and that he most wished his great grandfather Obadiah were there to relish them with him. He had a lot of work ahead of him, but still, he wanted to have the business finished within three days.

The morning after Mathers first made love with Jolene, he felt stranger than he ever had in his life. He was deeply in love with her, and thought she was with him, too. He should have been as happy as he'd ever been. But the specter of the murders loomed over this, just as it did over everything else in his life, and made it impossible for him to completely enjoy being in love. And the thought was still in the back of his mind that what seemed like love on her part might just be a desperate reaction to the terror that everyone in Breda felt because of the murders, and that was almost unbearable for anyone to face alone.

He'd talked to Quentin and Pursley about Jim finding out where Moses Kurtz had lived. They said they'd think about it and get back with him, but they hadn't yet. He wondered if they hadn't just laughed it off. After all, on the face of it, the idea a 95 year old man who lived over a thousand miles away could have anything to do with serial murders was absurd. And the idea of a Death

List was too hokey, too much like some late night horror show. But Mathers had a gut feeling there might be something to it. So even though he hated to leave, even though he would have preferred to drown himself in Jolene's love and forget all about the murders, he decided he'd better fly down to Florida himself to investigate. The fact he had the credentials of a police officer would mean that he could do a lot more than Jim had. Maybe he could get this Cowley to tell him where Moses Kurtz had been taken to. He picked his phone up and told Miss Ketchum, his secretary, to make the plane and hotel and car rental reservations. Whether he liked it or not, nothing was more important than trying to solve the murders. He just wished that Jim would call. He thought he would have heard something more from him by now. He wanted to talk to him again before he left for Florida.

When Jim woke up, his mind was still more in a state of sleep than consciousness, and he didn't remember where he was or how he'd gotten there. He wasn't even conscious of the mosquitoes that were sucking out his blood and that had been biting him for hours. It was only when he realized that, and swept them off his face and arms with his muddy hands, that everything started to come back to him. Maybe it was the surge of pain that shot through him when he moved his left arm that really woke him up. He could barely move it, and it felt like it was broken at the elbow. He slowly got up, amid the stench of the swamp, the buzz of mosquitoes, strange bird calls, and frogs croaking. A moment of panic went through him as he realized he had no idea which direction the road was in. The pasture and swamp seemed endless. All I can do, he thought, is walk in one direction and hope that sooner or later I'll come to a road or see a house. It was pitch dark. He saw no lights anywhere on the horizon. He wondered how long he'd lain there. An hour? A day? A week? He didn't have the slightest idea.

In almost every part of his body he felt pain, and he was so weakened that he could only move at a very slow pace. On top of everything else, he felt like he was starving. It wasn't so much hunger he felt, though—he was too sick to have any appetite—as the complete lack of energy a person feels and the emptiness in the stomach when he or she has gone far too long without food. After going only a short way, Jim started to feel faint and had to grab on to the trunk of a palmetto to keep from falling. After what seemed like hours but was really less than a half hour, Jim stopped and wondered if he'd really made any progress at all. The swamp he was in didn't look any different than the one he'd woke up in. He almost started to cry when he realized that he might even be farther from where he needed to go than when he'd started. Mosquitoes buzzed heavily around him, and he had to keep sweeping them off his face. But then he berated himself for being such a wimp and thought again how Julie's life might depend on his getting out of the swamp. So he pushed on. And after a while, instead of getting weaker, he at least thought he felt the slightest bit stronger. He finally made it out of the swamp, but all that lay ahead of him was a pasture full of cattle and beyond it another swamp. Continuing to walk straight ahead, he kept up the hope that sooner or later he had to come to a building with people in it.

After he had walked through the palm grove and swamp that was on the other side of the pasture, he came to another pasture, but on the far side of this pasture was a road and a house with lights on. He felt a tremendous surge of happiness, and a burst of energy carried him at almost a run to the house. He didn't stop to think how he'd be treated at the house—or even if anyone would be home, despite the lights being on—the house just seemed to him the most welcome sight he'd ever come across.

Even when he was on the porch of the house, and the reality of it had more of a chance to sink in, he didn't have any apprehension. It was only a day or so later that he realized how awful he must have looked and how lucky he was that the door wasn't just slammed in his face. He knocked on the door, and in a moment, it was opened by a pretty teenage girl with long, wavy blonde hair.

"My name is Jim Leiden." He paused because his mind was so clouded he wasn't sure what to say next. He realized he was barely audible. "I've been injured. I was wondering if I could come in and call the police."

And then he collapsed on the porch.

Chapter 11

Kurtz was more nervous about murdering Julie Veere than he'd been about any of his other victims. Certainly, this one involved the most risk. But he was so obsessed with it that nothing could have stopped him. And he was maybe slightly less worried about getting caught than he'd been at first, because he'd already done irreparable harm to Breda. Even if he were caught now, he'd have the satisfaction of knowing Breda had suffered harm from which it would likely never recover. He wasn't worried about a trial or prison. He carried with him at all times a cyanide tablet with a dosage strong enough to kill ten men, and if he were ever caught, he had every intention of swallowing it. The idea of death scared him less than the idea of a trial and prison.

At a costume store in Grand Rapids, he'd been able to pick up a fake beard that looked like the real thing and the clergyman's trademark black shirt with white collar. He'd also bought some foam rubber padding to fill himself out with, and he'd practiced the lines he was going to use as thoroughly as a Broadway actor. He wanted to wear sunglasses to hide his eyes, on just the off chance she might somehow recognize them. He was aware that people who saw his nearly black eyes rarely forgot them. But a clergyman wearing sunglasses at night was more likely to arouse suspicion than allay it, so he decided against it. He was still confident she wouldn't recognize him.

It was the night of the murder, and everything was in place. Kurtz chose eight o'clock as the time. Late enough so there would be few, if any, people in town, yet early enough so Julie would still be likely to come to the door. He drove to about a mile outside of town and walked the rest of the way, far away from the road so no one would notice him, in pasture and woods. One thing he didn't want around during the murder was his car, which would make it easy to identify him later. For all he knew, the cops might have everyone trained to write down the license plate numbers of strange vehicles. He carried the clergyman outfit in a grocery bag and would change when he got closer to Julie's house, ironically at a church nearby. It was a cold, crisp night with a half moon shrouded by a thin cloud and a few flurries falling. A few cars passed along the road, but Kurtz was sure no one in them saw him. When he got into town, a few more cars passed, but he didn't encounter anyone on the sidewalk. Everyone was locked and terrified in their houses. Luckily, he thought, no cops seem to be around at the moment.

When he got to the white Dutch Reformed church with the steeple at the outskirts of town, he went in back to the little cemetery to change. Right behind the church it was pitch dark, and he thought no one could possibly see him. It was eerily quiet there, with no sound but the flutter of leafless branches. Behind the church, the yard was filled with graves. Kurtz hoped there'd be another one to add to them before the night was over. He put his old clothes in the bag and put them in a garbage can that was against one wall of the church.

As he walked to Julie's house, he was more nervous, he thought, than he'd ever been in his life. He was practically shaking, and he wondered if he'd be able to keep his composure. Never had there been more at stake, and never had he put himself more at risk or had to use such a risky scheme. As he walked up the walkway to her door, he froze in doubt for a moment, even though he knew that every second he delayed increased the risk of someone seeing him or creating suspicion. Her porch light lit up his face as if it were midday. He had a terrible moment of doubt where this scheme that he'd spent weeks plotting out seemed the stupidest, most obvious idea he could have come up with and doomed to fail. But he also realized he was letting fear take over his thinking, and that he had to continue going forward with the plan. Never would there be a better time than now, he thought. No one has seen me, and I'm at her door. He let his mind fill again with his hatred of Breda and especially of Jim Leiden, because Leiden threatened to destroy everything Kurtz had planned, hoped, and schemed for. He thought of the consuming triumph he'd feel after Julie was killed, the devastation that Leiden would feel that would so shatter him that he would likely leave Breda and never be heard from again. Kurtz would be able to complete his Master Plan without having to constantly worry he was going to get caught.

He knocked on Julie's door. He heard a low, menacing bark from Kraut but nothing else for quite some time. He thought with bitterness what a devastating thing it would be if she weren't home, and he had to go through this again—if he even got the chance before Leiden talked to Moses and ruined everything. He knocked again, and still there was nothing. If she's home at all, she must be upstairs with her mother, he thought. Maybe she won't hear me, or maybe she doesn't answer the door at night anymore. Maybe she's seen me already and has called the police and is waiting for them to come! It seemed to him an eternity that he waited, and he almost left despite everything before she finally came to the door.

"Who are you and what do you want?" she said, without opening the door. He could see her, though, through the four small panes of glass on the door.

"I'm Reverend Phillip Winston of the Church of Christ," he said, in the soft, meek voice he'd practiced for days. "I was hoping you'd be willing to help out with our campaign to help abused children."

"I'm sure it's a good cause. But I don't open the door at night for anyone I don't know. I'm sure you know about the murders we've had in Breda. If you want, you can leave your name and address and any literature you might have in the mailbox."

She's only inches away, Kurtz thought! He realized he could pull out his gun and shoot her in the head if he was fast enough, but it would be noisy and messy, and he'd never get away.

"Yes, how kind of you," Kurtz said. "I may just do that."

Kurtz could see that Julie had a pistol in her hand and knew he didn't have a chance in the world.

"I'm sorry I have to do this, but we can't take chances in this town anymore. The people who took chances are dead now."

"Yes, yes. I understand."

Kurtz turned and walked away, but he could feel Julie's eyes watching him as if they were boring into him, and the image of the pistol was vividly in his mind. For the first time since before the first murder, he lost his composure and was nearly in a state of panic. Does she know I'm a fake, and will she call the police? he wondered. Does she recognize me? He wanted to run, but he knew that nothing would be more likely to call attention to himself, so he just kept walking like a zombie. Nearly paralyzed by fear and indecision, he imagined how it would be if the police caught him now. Of course, they wouldn't have anything on him immediately except impersonating a clergyman, and he wasn't even sure if that was a crime—except for asking for money. But at this point the cops were desperate. They'd use any excuse to search his house. They'd find the diaries that explained everything, they'd find Moses and talk to him. The whole game would be up. I'd be the most despised criminal in the annals of crime in Michigan, he thought.

He walked back to his car as briskly as he thought he could without arousing suspicion, his heart beating like it would burst from his chest. With every car that passed, he practically froze in fear, wondering who it was, and what they'd remember when the police went around asking everyone who they'd seen in Breda at that time of night. When a car came up so slowly behind him, he thought it was following him or trying to get a good look at him. He had trouble breathing and was afraid that his legs were going to give out from under him. Maybe they're going to get me now, he thought. Maybe the jig's finally up. If it were ever going to happen, that's the way he figured it would happen—completely unexpectedly. The car, a huge Pontiac of late '60s vintage, finally passed Kurtz, and he squinted to try to see who was inside. It was a family, a man and a woman in the front seat and a couple of goofy kids in back, but he couldn't make out who they were.

Finally, Kurtz got out of town back to the place where he could walk off the road into pastures and woods. He started feeling a little better, but he was still as nervous as if he'd drunk ten truck stop size cups of coffee. When he went through a cow pasture, the cows stared at him, and their eyes shined eerily in the moonlight like they were evil idols of some ancient culture. He started running, and when he finally got back to his car, he was breathing like he'd been on a treadmill all night. He started his car and started to drive away, but as luck would have it, a car quickly pulled up behind him, and he had to go through the fear and panic and intense anxiety he'd gone through on the walk back to the car all over again. But the car turned after a while, and finally Kurtz was alone again, on a country road all by himself.

He started berating himself for the stupidity of the failed plot. He couldn't believe he ever could have been stupid enough to think it would work, given all the precautions everyone had taken and what the cops must have told everyone. He'd let his overwhelming desire to kill Julie and wreak revenge on Jim Leiden get the better of his judgment. He'd come to think he was invincible. And because of it he'd made a major mistake.

Now the pigs will descend on the case like they never have before, he thought. Julie would tell them what had happened, they'd check and find out he was a fake, and then all hell would break loose. What a fool he'd been for even giving her a name! That would make it so easy to prove he was phony! For the first time, the cops would really be able to smell blood, and they'd go after it like sharks. Even if he did escape being caught, he'd never be able to operate so close to Breda anymore, and he'd have to leave tonight. The pigs will probably question everyone within a hundred mile radius that looks even remotely like me. He thought of the people who lived nearby him and who might have seen him enough to make a connection between the description Julie would give the police and what he looked like. Surely the Nickelsons, he thought, and their ugly brood would try to stick their noses in it. They were nearly across the street, although both houses were set quite a ways back from the road. Or would his disguise and beard make it impossible for anyone to identify him?

That Julie had foiled Kurtz's attempt to kill her only made him hate her more. Far from lessening his desire to kill her, his failure to do so the first time increased his obsession with killing her. He'd go to any length now to kill her. His desire to kill her was so great he could hardly think of anything else. It possessed his mind night and day. Next time, though, he thought, I won't try anything that risky. Next time he'd cut her down with a sniper's bullet or something else that was sure to work. He also decided it would be his last killing before the grand finale—blowing up the elementary school when it was filled with kids—that would utterly waste Breda. Time was no longer on his side. Jim Leiden was prowling around Florida and had got who knows what cops to help him out. Sooner or later they'd find Moses Kurtz and the stupid old man would be sure to talk.

Jim kept telling himself how lucky he was to have stopped at a house that had such a nice, friendly family living in it. Instead of treating him like a nut or a bum, they'd taken him to a doctor and made him a hot meal, and though he hadn't been able to eat much of it, he'd gone to bed and slept about 14 hours. He had a lot of aches and pains, but amazingly, his arm wasn't broken, just badly strained. His car had been found right where he'd left it.

Jim couldn't do much of anything besides lie in bed and eat the day he was at the Cuylers. He thought a lot about why the guys who'd beat him up hadn't killed him. It seemed like killing him would have made so much more sense. Now he'd be able to talk. Maybe he really had convinced them that the cops were on to Cowley, and if they killed him, they could be tried for murder. Or maybe their orders had just been to rough him up enough to keep him away. Did they believe he was dead? Maybe they were just amateurs. The local deputy who came out didn't know what to make of it. All he'd really done is make out a report and leave. The fact was that Jim didn't have any hard evidence for the police to go on, just suspicions. He couldn't prove the goons in the blue Chevy had been set on him by Cowley. He didn't even have its license number or know what state it was from.

The next day, Jim woke up feeling much better and decided it was time to leave. He sat down to a breakfast of fried eggs, bacon, hash brown potatoes, and grits. Andy Cuyler, the father, was out working the farm with the two boys. June Cuyler, the mother, was cleaning up breakfast. Jim sat at the kitchen table with Mandy Cuyler, Andy and June's sixteen year old daughter.

"That's jest lak somethin' out of a book or a horror movie, ain't it, Mom?" Mandy said, about the murders in Breda and what Jim told her he'd done to try to find the killers.

Mandy was a little plump but had a nice tan and lovely big green eyes. Jim thought she really had the look of a Southern girl, though he couldn't exactly have said why. She seemed to have a bit of a crush on him and hung on his every word as he told her the story. June didn't answer for a moment, as if she'd only half been listening as she worked.

"Oh, yes, it's awful all raght. We're so lucky we've never had anything lak that happen in Dothan."

"The sheriff of my county is down here, and I'm going to try to meet up with him this afternoon," Jim said, just before eating another spoonful of grits.

"Ah'd go with you maself if Mom'd let me," looking over at her mother.

"Don't be silly, Mandy. The last thing those men would want is a silly teenage girl tagging along after them when they're trying to solve a murder."

"I can't tell you how grateful I am that you took me in. I could have died out there—I sure felt like it."

"We weren't sure what to think when you came to the door," June said. "But somehow you looked lak someone we could trust. You've got an honest face, Ah suppose."

Jim smiled. "Not everyone would agree with you on that."

After breakfast, Jim left for the Ramada Inn in Orlando where Mathers had booked a room. After calling Mathers' office, Jim had been able to locate him, and they'd talked on the phone. Mathers met Jim in the lobby of the motel.

"Well, well, you look like you've been beat up and have the measles to boot," Mathers said. "Those guys really got you, didn't they?"

"They sure did," Jim said. "Luckily they didn't do any permanent damage. Some mosquitoes had themselves a party, though."

"That's really something about Julie, isn't it?"

"It just blew me away. I still can't quite get over it."

"We checked up on the so-called clergyman. As it turns out, there is no Phillip Winston ordained in Michigan in the church he said he was from. We don't know for sure, of course, but we're assuming it was the killer."

"Let's go to your room right now, so I can try calling her again. When she told me about it yesterday, I was still too out of it to talk to her about it much."

As soon as Mathers opened the door, Jim went to the phone and called Julie back. Mathers stayed outside so Jim could talk alone.

"Hi, Honey! I just wanted to hear your voice again. Mathers is with me here in Orlando. We were talking about that phony minister. It scares the hell out of me every time I think about it."

"It scared the hell out of me at the time. But somehow, now that I've actually seen this guy, I'm not scared as much. He's a real runt. He'll probably avoid me like the plague now, since I'm the one person who's seen him. We're all assuming he's the killer, but of course no one knows that for sure. He could really just be a con man out looking to make some spare change. I'm less worried about that right now, though, then I am about you. How are you?"

"I'm fine. I'm a hundred percent better today. I just wish I could be back there with you. I've really gotten sick of it down here, and I can't wait to get back. I'll stay down here with Mathers for a couple of days, and if we still haven't found Moses Kurtz, I'm coming back no matter what. I love you a ton, kid."

"I love you, too, and I really miss you. Just don't worry about me while you're down there."

"You know better than to think I could ever do that, but I'll try to put a lid on it, now that I know you outfoxed the fox himself."

"If that's what he was. Only the killer knows for sure."

As soon as Jim got off the phone, he went outside, where he found Mathers standing by a garden not far from the room.

"Nice weather they've got down here," Mathers said. "If I didn't have work to do, I'd stay awhile."

He'd been imagining making love with Jolene in a house by the beach that was off by itself surrounded by palm trees. Maybe someday, he thought, if this madness ever ends.

"So what's our next move?" Jim said.

"As soon as I get settled in, we're going to see a police detective I talked to on the phone before I left. There was an article in the *St. Petersburg Times* about the murders recently, and now everyone down here is talking about them again."

Within an hour they were at the Orlando Field Office of the Bureau of Criminal Investigations and Intelligence, in the office of Inspector Bobby Jackson. Jackson looked at Jim kind of funny because of how beat up he looked, and Mathers explained why he'd brought him along.

"We got an anonymous tip in here today that maght be of some hep," Jackson said with a thick accent. "Somebody called in and said there's a man named Moses Kurtz living in an old folks' home called Golden Garden in Petula who knows about the murders. That's the man you said you were lookin' for down here."

This was so unexpected that both Mathers and Jim were speechless for a moment. The article in the *St. Petersburg Times* had apparently given them a huge assist. Before now, for Jim it was almost like Moses Kurtz wasn't even a real person, was just a figment of his imagination, and that it wasn't possible that he could really exist. Now that he might actually get a chance to talk to him, Jim didn't know what to say.

"If you know where the place is, I'd like you to take us there as quickly as you can," Mathers said. "I really think the guy might know something."

"We can leave raght now if you'd lak. Ah'll have Gertrude git us some coffee for the road."

As it turned out, Petula was about an hour's drive from Orlando. Mathers and Inspector Jackson talked quite a bit about the case, but Jim hardly said a word. All he could think about was what it would be like talking to Moses Kurtz, what he would look like, what he would say. Jim was worried, too, that he would be gone by the time they got there, that he would have been moved again just like he had been from the Shady Palms.

The Golden Garden turned out to be out in the middle of nowhere—a perfect place to hide someone. The home itself was pretty rundown but was in a lovely setting of live oaks draped with Spanish moss. An older black woman with straightened hair was working the front desk. Her nameplate read Arlene Richmond.

"Inspector Jackson of the state police," Jackson said to her. "Ah'd lak to speak to Moses Kurtz."

She looked surprised, as if to say, why would the police ever be interested in talking to an old man like that? Jim wondered who had called the police about Moses.

"He's in room 216, sir," Arlene said. "He should be in there now. We'll be servin' him dinner there in about fifteen minutes."

She paused and looked like she was trying to remember something.

"Ah'd better have you talk to the manager, Mr. Ross, before you go up."

She called for Mr. Ross on an intercom, and shortly he appeared in the reception area. He was a short, pudgy man in his late 30s or so, quite bald, with large, nondescript features. But Jim thought from his eyes that he looked intelligent.

"What's the problem, gentlemen?" he said after he'd introduced himself.

"We'd lak to talk to one of your residents, Mr. Moses Kurtz," Jackson said.

Ross looked surprised.

"Don't try to figure it out," Mathers said. "Just take us to his room."

Jim thought it surprising the Kurtzes didn't at least have Moses registered under a phony name. It must be that he wouldn't have gone along with it, he thought, or that some ID had to be shown to register him. Apparently, the staff at the Golden Garden wasn't in on any kind of scheme to hide Moses.

Jim didn't think he'd ever felt more anticipation than he did as they waited for the elevator that would take them to the second floor, and as they walked down the corridor to room 216. When Ross opened the door, they saw Moses Kurtz lying in bed. It was a hospital type bed and he was propped up at about a 45 degree angle. His eyes moved a little, but other than that, he didn't even seem to notice that anyone had come into the room.

"Mr. Kurtz, these men have come here to talk to you," Ross said. "This is Inspector Bobby Jackson, Sheriff Bill Mathers, and Jim Leiden."

Moses turned his head just slightly toward them but didn't speak. He was so pale and shriveled Jim would have believed it if he'd been told he wasn't expected to live more than another day. He had only the slightest wisp of hair left, and his veins showed through his skin. He seemed to Jim more dead than alive.

"Mr. Kurtz, there's been some murders up in Michigan in a town called Breda," Inspector Jackson said. "We think you may have somethin' to tell us about them."

Moses moved his head slightly, but Jim couldn't have said for sure whether it was a nod or not. Jackson looked at Ross as if to say, can this man still talk or is he already beyond that?

"We think someone in your family is killing people in Breda to get revenge because your father was hanged in Breda," Mathers said. "But we don't want to see any more people die, and we don't think you want that either. Innocent people are dying who had nothing to do with killing your father."

A pained look came into the old man's eyes, and Jim wasn't sure whether it was from fear or because of the way he felt about the killings. But at that moment, Jim was sure that he did know something about them.

"He can still talk, can't he?" Mathers said to Ross. Ross nodded.

"It's my grandnephew done it," Moses Kurtz said in a whispery, gravelly voice, and suddenly every eye was glued to him, and everyone else was silent. He seemed like he was about to cry. "Hinton, all he ever cared about was Pop, all the humiliation they put him through, hanging him for nothing." He paused, like he needed to gather his strength before going on. "He took it real serious, even when he was a kid when he heard the story about it for the first time. And when Hinty lived in Breda when he was a boy, all the other kids hated him 'cause of the way he looked."

Slowly, he brought a bony arm up to cover his face and closed his eyes. Jim could sense the agony he was going through and felt bad for him. No one said anything to him for quite a while.

"How do you know he committed the murders?" Mathers said.

"'Cause he told me. Not in so many words. But he told me he was going to get terrible revenge on Breda."

"If you could tell us where we could find him, you might be able to save innocent people from dying," Mathers finally said. "Anything you can tell us might help."

"I don't rightly know anymore. He hasn't called me or come to see me in a long time. But I know he's the one who done it. I just found out about the murders a coupla days ago. Someone was readin' the paper real loud." He paused again. "He was living out in the country somewhere last I knew. Never gave me no address."

It was clear to Mathers they weren't likely to get any more useful information from Moses, and the last thing he wanted to do was torment him any more than he had to.

"Is there anything more you'd like to tell us before we leave, Mr. Kurtz?" Mathers said.

"Go easy on the boy. He don't know what he's doing. He ain't right in the head. Never was."

Mathers nodded. "Thank you very much, Mr. Kurtz. You may have helped save a lot of lives."

They turned to walk away, but Jim's gaze stayed on Moses longer than the others. Thoughts crowded into his mind. Everything he'd ever thought about the murders seemed to come into his mind at once. For a moment just before Jim turned away, he and Moses looked right into each other's eyes. Jim felt a chill go through him. Surely, he thought, the image of that moment would be with him the rest of his life. He'd waited so long to talk to Moses Kurtz and spent so many hours imagining it, it was hard for him to come to grips with it actually happening. It would always seem to him more a dream than real.

They went downstairs to the lobby to talk further to Mr. Ross.

"Did a man named Hinton Kurtz bring Moses Kurtz here to live?" Mathers asked him.

"I think that was his name. I'll check our records to be sure."

"Why don't you do that," Jackson said.

Ross went into an office and returned shortly.

"Yes, that was the name," Ross said. "He listed an address in Breda, Michigan. He's thin and a little bent over like he has some kind of deformity, but his arms look really strong, like he's been lifting weights for a long time. The thing I remember about him most is his eyes. They're the darkest eyes I've ever seen, and cruel. He tried not to let anyone look him in the eye. When you see him, he's the kind of guy you wouldn't trust as far as you could throw him."

Mathers got up and went to the phone at the front desk. He dialed Quentin at the Michigan State Police post in Grand Rapids.

"I think we got our boy, Ken," he said. "I just talked to a man named Moses Kurtz living in an old folks home down here. He says his grandnephew, Hinton Kurtz, is the Breda Killer. He doesn't know where he's living other than that he thinks he's living out in the country somewhere. But I'm sure your boys can find him. The old folks home has an address for him, but it's probably phony."

"You're shittin' me," Quentin said. "Are you sure you know what in the hell you're doing?"

"Yeah, you son-of-a-bitch. Do you want to go pick up Hinton Kurtz or would you rather wait until he kills some more people?"

"All right. We'll go look for him. But there better be something to this."

"Thanks, Jackson," Mathers said when he got off the phone. "I'm going to go back to Michigan just as fast as I can get a plane to take me there. I'm sure Mr. Ross here will see to it that Moses Kurtz isn't moved again, won't you, Mr. Ross?"

"I never had anything to do with moving him in the first place," Ross said angrily. "And, frankly, I resent any other implication."

"Don't git so hot under the collar," Jackson said. "Nobody's accused you of anythang."

"Jim, I assume you're going to drive back to Breda more or less without stopping. I'm sure you want to get back and see Julie as fast as you can. I'd take you back with me if I thought there was someplace on the plane to put that car of yours," smiling.

"Don't worry about it," Jim said. "I'll be back there in a day, and that's good enough. You probably won't beat me by much by the time you get done fooling around at airports."

Chapter 12

Jim got directions from Lt. Jackson on the quickest way to get to I-75 and left immediately for home. He made his first stop for gas just across the Florida line at Valdosta, Georgia, and called Julie from a phone booth there to tell her he was on his way. As he drove, he got more and more anxious to be home, felt more uneasy about being away, and he thought a lot about how vulnerable Julie—or anybody, for that matter—was to Hinton Kurtz.

With so much idle time on his hands to just think, terrible visions preyed on Jim's mind. No matter how hard he tried to stop them, images of Julie being murdered or lying in her house in a pool of blood kept flashing into his mind. He imagined her being knifed, shot, and strangled. He saw the letters ZOSO written on her waist. Throughout the ordeal of the murders, he'd been like a rock of stability compared to most, but he thought that maybe he'd tried too hard to maintain a façade of normality and coolness. Now that the ordeal was perhaps nearly over, now that the murderer was maybe only hours or days away from being captured, the floodgates of his psyche seemed to be opening and allowing in the worst nightmares he could have imagined. It made him feel sick to his stomach, and he completely lost any appetite. He knew he should stop for food because he needed to keep up his energy for the long drive ahead, but he didn't think he could even force himself to eat.

Jim became obsessed with the idea that the killer would try again to kill Julie, that she'd been marked down by him as his next victim, and that he'd failed in his first attempt would only make him redouble his effort. He had a feeling of utter helplessness, because part of his nightmare was that he wouldn't get back in time to be able to stop her murder. He imagined the murderer having a kind of omniscience, that he would know he had to kill Julie before Jim got back and fully intended to do so. Such thoughts Jim tried to fight off with that side of him that was still rational. He recalled his conversation with Julie from Valdosta and tried to tell himself how tremendous the odds were against her being killed in just the 16 hours or so it would take him to get back to Breda. He tried listening to a rock station on the radio and then switched to a station with a minister preaching fire and brimstone, but he couldn't get his mind off Julie. If anything, the apocalyptic rantings of the minister only increased his apprehension.

"Take heed, sinnas," the minister said, in a wildly emotional voice with a thick Southern accent. "The day of judgment is comin' soon. And how many of you can say you are ready? How many of you can say your lives aren't blackened ba sin?" his voice rising. "How many can say they haven't rejected the glorious mercy of the Lord?"

Jim finally turned the radio off. The songs annoyed him, and he didn't want to hear anyone talk. When he got to Chattanooga, it was 11 pm, the latest he figured he could call Julie without either waking her up or scaring the shit out of her. He stopped at a truck stop and looked around for a pay phone to call her from. He spotted one in a corner amid cheap souvenirs adorned with confederate flags and landmarks of the state of Tennessee. The stools at the grill were filled with guys who looked like they were born to drive trucks.

When Jim heard Julie's voice, a tremendous feeling of relief flowed all through him.

"Oh, hi, Jim," she said. "I didn't think I'd hear from you again until you were home."

"I've been real worried about you," Jim said. "With all this driving, I guess I've just got too much time to think."

"Don't be silly, Babe. I'm doing just fine. The killer will be caught soon, and we'll all be able to go back to leading normal lives. Either that or he got so scared after he botched trying to kill me that he's gone as far away from here as he can, never to be seen again."

"I hope you're right, Jules. I can't wait to get back to see you again."

"I second that emotion. I'll see you soon, love. Just don't push yourself too hard on the road. Stop somewhere and sleep for a while. I'll sleep a lot better if I know you're going to."

"I'll stop if I get tired. But to tell you the truth, the last thing on my mind right now is sleep. I'm not a bit tired."

"Just be sure you stop if you do get tired. In any case, I'll see you tomorrow sometime."

Jim felt a lot better after the call, but as soon as he got back in the cocoon of his car, horrible thoughts started to prey on his mind again. He got tired fast after about 1 am, and his mind seemed to drift off half into dreamland. He finally got to where he could hardly keep his eyes open, and he knew he'd have to stop. He got off the freeway at the next rest area he came to and laid down to try to sleep. When he woke up, it was still dark. Somehow he'd been able to sleep a few hours, and he felt much better. He thought now that maybe the lack of sleep had been responsible for the terrible thoughts he'd had, and that if he'd have been smart, he'd have stopped earlier.

So instead of murder and blood, when he got back on the road, his head filled with pleasant images, of looking into Julie's eyes and making love with her and holding her close in bed.

The more time that passed after Kurtz's foiled attempt to kill Julie, the more rage he felt. And not only that. As time went on, he began to direct the rage less and less on himself and more on her. He came to see her as his archenemy, out to destroy him and the Master Plan he'd crafted so carefully. He came to think it would be worth anything, taking any risk to kill her. He was ready to throw all caution to the wind. As it had with his feelings about Obadiah, his hatred for Julie and his thirst for vengeance grew upon themselves, snowballed until he could think of almost nothing else.

It was in such a state that he sat at a window of the unpainted shack that he'd rented for $100 a month in Leerton, which was about a hundred miles north of Breda. He figured he was just beyond the danger zone now that the cops were scouring the whole area around Breda looking for the phony minister. It was late afternoon, and he sat in his rocking chair with no lights on and little heat, staring out the window. Snow swirled, and the wind whined as a storm began. Kurtz had heard on the radio that a foot or more of snow was expected to fall during the next day.

He smiled a little as he thought how really easy it is to kill someone if you don't care about getting caught. It gave him comfort to know that if he *really* wanted to kill Julie Veere, he could do it. There was no question about that, he thought. Then like a lightning bolt, the thought flashed through his mind that a snowstorm could very well be the perfect time to execute a murder. No pun intended, he thought with a smile. If the snowstorm were bad enough, visibility would be reduced to virtually zero. He'd be able to move around Breda like the Invisible Man. As the beauty of it became apparent to him, he smiled and then laughed, and practically wanted to pat himself on the back.

The swish and whine of the snow and the wind seemed like music to him. Now there was just the matter of a plan. The first thing that came into his mind was how handy it might be to cut Julie's telephone line—and all hope of communication. What with the phone company running all over the county trying to keep up with all the downed lines the storm would cause, it might be days before they got around to Julie. He decided he'd kill her in the middle of the night. Three or four o'clock would be perfect.

Night and snow. The perfect combination for murder, he thought with a laugh. With the noise of the snow and wind, she wouldn't even be able to hear him jimmy the lock on the back door. There'd be the matter of the dog to contend with, but mace and a knife would take care of him. He'd bring a flashlight to see his way around, then go up to her bedroom and shine it in her face as he stabbed her to death. As he imagined the look of terror on her face just before he killed her, he felt tremendous exhilaration, almost an erotic feeling.

Kurtz had everything he needed to carry out the murder. Now it was just a matter of the weather cooperating. The thought of that moved him to turn on a light and the old beat-up radio that sat on a table against the wall. He wanted to reaffirm the forecast he'd only casually listened to before. Reception was weak and scratchy because of the storm and how far away the stations were, but Kurtz was able to find a station that came through pretty clearly. It annoyed him immensely, though, to have to listen to songs like "Sugar, Sugar" by the Archies and "One, Two, Three Red Light" by the 1910 Fruitgum Company as he waited for a weather forecast. The wait seemed interminable after a while, and he began to wonder whether this station had given its last forecast of the night. At one point, he nearly picked up the radio and smashed it on the floor. He was almost ready to give up when the news came on and then the weather.

"We interrupt this broadcast for the following bulletin: The National Weather Service was issued a severe winter storm warning for all counties in the western Lower Peninsula," the announcer said. "Blizzard conditions are to be expected, with blowing and drifting, accompanied by accumulations of up to 16 inches of snow in some places. The state police are warning motorists to stay home except in case of extreme emergency. The storm is expected to continue through tonight and on into tomorrow."

Well, thought Kurtz, I guess we have an extreme emergency on our hands, don't we? And he laughed uproariously.

Jim was just past the Indiana line when something happened that he hadn't thought of in all the scenarios he'd gone through in his head of what the trip would be like, even though it wasn't anything remarkable. Snow began to fall. At first the snowfall was light and only made Jim a little nervous. Visibility was still decent, and the snow swept across the road without building up or icing the road. He was hardly past Indianapolis, though, before it picked up markedly and blew and swirled heavily enough so that he had to slow down to about 45 miles an hour. He swore and slammed his hand on the steering wheel in anger. The last thing he wanted was to get stopped by a snowstorm and have to wait another day to get home. Then he heard the prediction of a severe winter snowstorm on the radio but decided he would keep driving at all costs unless his car was brought to a complete stop.

Other headlights and taillights thinned out before long to a point where he often went five minutes or more without seeing another car. Then it seemed like he was the only one on the road, in complete isolation, with only the sound of the radio and the wind. He was down to about 25 miles per hour and was getting scared. He started to rethink his situation. The worst thing that could happen, he thought, was to get stuck and die in the snow. In a storm like this, I could lie dead in the snow for days before anyone found me. He decided he might have to break down and stop after all. But he wanted to at least call Julie first. He was fortunate he came to an exit in just a couple of miles.

He pulled into a Grandma's restaurant that was just off the exit and went inside. A half dozen people were in the restaurant. He had the feeling they'd all been talking together and just stopped and stared at him when he walked in. Even after just the short walk from his car, the snow was coming down so hard, and the wind was blowing so hard, he thought he must look to them like the Abominable Snowman.

"Is there a public phone here?" Jim said.

"On your left," the waitress who was standing behind the counter said. She was fiftyish, gruff, and seemed wary, as if only regulars were in the restaurant, and Jim had interrupted a pleasant conversation.

"I didn't see it."

It was practically within reach from where he stood. He dialed the operator and asked to make a collect call to Julie.

"I'm sorry, that number is out of service," the operator said, her voice sounding as eerie and distant as if she'd been on the moon.

"That's impossible. I just called it yesterday," suddenly realizing that he was talking way too loud.

"I couldn't make a connection. Let me try again."

After maybe thirty seconds that seemed much longer to Jim, the operator came on the line.

"I'm sorry, I still can't get through. Try again later."

Jim was left holding the phone. He stared at it and then finally slammed it back on the hook. He'd almost forgotten about the people in the restaurant, but he suddenly realized they were all staring at him.

"I couldn't get through," Jim said.

"Wouldn't surprise me if half the lines from here to Canada were out," an old man sitting at the counter said.

"It was really an important call. I really needed to get through."

The old man nodded.

"You ain't thinking of goin' back out there again, are you?"

"I have to. I have to get home. I can't wait another day. If I wait, I could end up being stuck here for a week."

"'Taint so bad here, really. If you go back out there, you're liable to be stuck here forever. Or at least until spring when they find your bones in a ditch somewhere."

"A person would have to be crazy to go out there," the waitress said. "Look at it."

It was snowing so hard Jim couldn't even see his car. "I'd love to stay. I really would," with a note of sarcasm. "But I have to go. Now more than ever."

He turned away, trying to avoid looking into anyone's eyes, though he thought he could feel their eyes staring through him.

"Good luck," the old man said. "You'll need a lot of damn fool luck where you're going. I'll look for your name in the paper. The obituary section."

With that cheery thought, Jim stepped out the door into a world that felt to him like a different dimension.

The people in the restaurant already seemed like a figment of his imagination. He felt like he was the only human on a strange planet. It wasn't easy finding his car, and as soon as he started driving again, he had the same feeling of cosmic isolation that he'd felt earlier. If anything, too, he had to drive even slower than he had before he'd stopped. He just crawled along at 15 to 20 miles per hour. He tried to calculate how long it would take him to get back to Breda at that rate, but he gave it up when more horrible images of Julie being murdered began to flood into his brain again.

He imagined her throat being cut and blood pouring out. He imagined her being choked with a rope. He imagined her being riddled by bullets. Nothing he could do could block those images from his mind. He thought he was being mesmerized by the snow and remembered a story he'd read about snow madness, about how people trapped in a blizzard could temporarily lose their sanity.

If Jim weren't on the road, the snowstorm wouldn't have bothered Julie at all. At least not at first. The isolation that it made her feel was actually welcome after all the worrying she'd done about the Breda Killer, and it was comforting for her to know that within a day Jim would be home, and she'd have him to hold all night long. She just hoped Jim had sense enough to stop at a motel and wait for the storm to break and the roads to be cleared. She doubted he had, though, because she figured the first thing he'd do if he stopped would be to call her. After a while, she got to thinking this was one of the worst snowstorms she'd ever been through. It was starting to bother her, so she decided she'd call a couple of friends, so she could assure herself there was still a world left outside her door. But when she picked up the phone, she found the line was dead. At times she stayed glued to her TV, mesmerized by the reports about the storm. The weatherman on the station she was watching she thought looked like a Ken doll, as he cheerfully predicted that the storm would be one of record breaking severity. The governor was thinking about sending out the National Guard. Julie started to worry about a power outage. If one hit, the temperature in the house would plummet. She doubted her mother would survive long if the temperature dropped very far, and the snowstorm was so bad, she doubted she'd be able to take her anywhere.

She went upstairs to check on her. As she suspected, her mother hadn't been able to fall asleep. She was sitting up in bed, wraithlike but with a sweet looking face, reading a *Readers Digest*. Julie sat on the bed beside her and held her hand.

"Pretty hard to sleep with all the racket the storm's making, isn't it?" Julie said.

"It surely is, dear," Bonnie Veere said. "I was just thinking back to a terrible snowstorm we had back in '28. It was so cold we had to stay up all night by the wood stove to keep from freezing. In some ways storms weren't as bad as now, though. We didn't have a phone or central heating yet out in the country where we lived. Everything we had we depended on ourselves for."

"Hopefully this thing will blow over before too much longer," though she knew from listening to the weather forecasts that wasn't likely. "It hardly seems possible the clouds could hold much more snow."

The Strange Curse of Breda

Her mother laughed.

"There's no end to how much snow God can put in the sky."

Julie was glad to see her mother in such good spirits, but when she left her and went back downstairs, she couldn't help but worry more and more about what the storm might bring. She'd go to bed soon, but she knew she wouldn't sleep well.

Kurtz went to bed early so he could get a few hours' sleep but had a hard time falling asleep. All he could think about was his murder plan. He alternated between ecstasy as he imagined carrying out the murder successfully and intense concentration as he tried to work out the last details to perfection. He lay curled up in bed in pitch dark thinking it all out and listening to the wind blow the snow against the house. He tried to think of what else he needed to do to get ready. He had a knife, a .38 pistol, ammunition, and wire cutters laid out. The flashlight was in the car. Nothing was left to do but get up and go.

Kurtz finally did doze off and needed the alarm to wake him up at midnight. He felt terrible and had a hard time dragging himself out of bed. He swore at himself for not just staying up. He practically felt sick, and his mind felt like it was full of cotton at a time he needed it to be razor sharp. But he figured he'd feel fine by the time he got to Breda. He had a long way to go. Within minutes he'd dressed and put everything he'd need in the big pockets of his parka.

When he stepped outside, though, he was shocked. He'd thought of the weather as a friend, but the storm was so bad and had gone on so long, he wasn't sure he'd be able to go anywhere now. The Jeep he'd bought to replace his car after he'd moved away from Breda was practically buried in snow. When he shined the flashlight on it, about all he could see was part of the windshield and side windows. He swore and went back inside to get a broom to sweep it off with.

When that was done, he got in to leave, but the snow was so deep he was barely able to get the Jeep out of the driveway—even with four wheel drive. He started down the road but had to drive so slowly, he thought he'd almost be better off walking. Of all the stupid ass things, he thought. Why in the hell did I wait so long to leave? Now what the hell time will I get there? Nine o'clock in the morning? After the goddamn sun has already come out? Why not just drive to the goddamn pig station and turn myself in? Fuck! You'll never make it now, you asshole!

He went on berating himself for being so stupid for not taking into account how bad the storm could get and how much it could slow him down. But he doggedly kept on driving. If there was any chance at all of carrying out the murder that night, he was going to do it. The idea of delaying it was more than he could stand. He just had to hope that at some point he'd come to a road that had been cleared, and he could drive faster. He just wondered if he wouldn't eventually come to a snowdrift that was so high he wouldn't be able to get past it.

He turned on the radio, hoping for weather news, but the first thing that came on was "Sugar, Sugar" again, and he was so upset that he practically tore the knobs off the radio. But he kept the radio on. Almost any voice was preferable to the terrible and deathly isolation of a midnight blizzard. If anything, the ferocity of the storm increased as he drove. He felt after a while that he didn't really know where he was any more. Any attempt to read road signs was fruitless. But he was pretty sure he was driving in the right direction, so he kept on. He turned on a news station but didn't really even hear the words. Even the news about the blizzard barely dented his consciousness. Fear started to grip him as he realized that now not only was the murder a chancy proposition, but he might even be lucky to even survive the storm if it didn't let up soon.

After driving what seemed like forever, Kurtz got out at an intersection to try to find a road sign, even though he hated to and didn't feel completely safe going even ten feet from his Jeep. He felt his way around until he found the pole and was eventually able to read the "L Avenue" and "34th Street" signs at the top of it. Thanks to the grid system that's used in most rural counties in Michigan, he now knew exactly where he was, and as it turned out, he'd gone farther than he'd thought. He wasn't all that far from I-196, but he knew he'd have to stick to back roads if he wanted to avoid contact with the police or the National Guard. He checked his watch. It was 2 am. He figured he had about three hours to get to Breda, kill Julie, and get out of town. He believed now that he could make it, and a smile came to his lips as he thought about how close he was to his goal. He wasn't scared of the storm anymore.

Chapter 13

By four o'clock Kurtz was on the outskirts of Breda, and the storm still hadn't let up a bit. He stopped to go over his final strategy, though he knew he didn't have much time for planning and thinking. People would start waking up soon, so he had to work fast. He wanted practically to be back at his house by sunrise. He was mentally exhausted from driving through the storm and extremely tired, but his obsession with murdering Julie kept him going, kept his adrenaline up enough to go the last mile of his plan.

With snow swirling around his Jeep in pitch darkness, he sat and thought. He'd park a block from Julie's house—it wouldn't hurt to be close because of the dark and the snow—and walk into her back yard to cut the telephone lines. Then he'd jimmy the lock on the back door. Her dog would be there, and he'd mace him and then stab him, get him out of the way as quickly and quietly as possible. That would be the most difficult part. If the dog made too much of a racket, Julie might wake up, and she could come down with her gun. But if the dog did start barking, Kurtz hoped Julie would think it was just the storm that set him off. Once I'm in the house and the dog's out of the way, I'll sneak upstairs and kill Julie and her mother too for good measure, Kurtz thought, chuckling. With that thought he put his foot on back on the gas pedal. He was suddenly jolted, though, and found that he was stuck in a snowdrift. All he could do was get the wheels of the Jeep to spin helplessly. The snow was just too deep, and no one else had been on the road to clear a lane. Now that he'd lost his momentum, the Jeep wouldn't move.

"Of all the fucking bad luck," he said. "Worst possible thing that could happen!"

He got out with his flashlight to take a look. His Jeep was so far off the ground it could have been on a hoist. Not only that. The cold wind pierced through him so quickly he felt like someone had stabbed him with a pitchfork made of ice. The only way he could survive in that kind of cold was to keep moving. He decided he had to find a log or something else that he could put under the tires for them to grip onto. He walked around the field next to the Jeep for a few minutes but couldn't find anything that was even close to adequate. It was difficult to even walk in the snow. He was close to a state of panic. He got back in the Jeep. He couldn't do anything or go anyplace without the Jeep. Everything depended on it. Considering the ferocity of the storm, he probably couldn't even survive long outside it. Even just the few minutes he'd spent outside it had chilled him to the bone and practically worn him out. He was near the end of his rope. Only the fury of his hate kept him going. He rocked the Jeep back and forth and back and forth and back and forth, and finally, just barely, he was able to get the tires of the Jeep out of the rut they were in and get it moving again. He was too exhausted to feel elated, though. All the mental and emotional energy he had left was focused on carrying out the murder. And he was very aware that the time he had left to commit the murder and get out of town was ticking down fast.

He'd no sooner got going again, though, than he thought he saw a pair of headlights behind him. It was just the faintest light, and he wasn't entirely sure if it was really headlights or just an optical illusion or figment of his exhausted brain. As he drove the mile or so he had left, the lights didn't seem to get any closer or define themselves any better, but they still left him edgy and scared. He figured nine chances out of ten were that any vehicle on the road now would be a cop or a National Guardsman, and they'd be sure to stop him if they came up behind him.

When Kurtz was about a block from Julie's house, he stopped at a spot where the snow wasn't as deep as it was most places. The lights behind him—or whatever they were—had disappeared. He checked the big pockets of his parka for the knife, gun, mace, wire cutters, flashlight, and crowbar. He put his ski mask over his face and started walking. He could barely breathe and barely see. He might well have been exploring Antarctica. He wasn't long out of the Jeep when he began to wonder if he really had parked where he thought he had. He had felt certain that he had stopped at the corner of Main Street and Felter, but now he wasn't so sure. He knew if he wasn't careful he could easily get lost. He had to expend a great deal of effort to walk through the snow. All the fears and worries he'd had about the murder started to multiply, and during certain moments, he felt close to panic. Yet he still kept moving forward as inexorably as a robot. Now, nothing could have kept him from trying to carry out the murder.

It seemed like an eternity, but Kurtz finally found Julie's house. Being that close gave him a surge of new energy. He could see himself in the house holding the knife in front of a terrified Julie Veere. A warm feeling went through him like it was a summer day. When he got to the back of the house and got back to the practical business of carrying out the murder, though, he was met with another problem. He couldn't find the telephone line coming out of the house so he could cut it. He didn't linger over that long, though. Considering the ferocity of the storm, he thought the last thing he'd have to worry about was Julie calling someone and their having time to get to the house before she was dead, and he was long gone.

He went to the back door. It was a double door. He used the crowbar to jam open the outer door, then broke one of the little panes on the inner door and reached through it to open it. He wasn't worried about the noise. The wind was making so much noise, he figured the noise of the glass breaking probably couldn't have been heard for more than five feet.

With his flashlight on, Kurtz walked towards the stairs that led up to the bedrooms. He wondered where the dog was. Must be in her bedroom, he thought. That presented a new wrinkle, but it didn't bother him. He'd just shoot him and then go after Julie. He was nervous and scared. It was all real now. No more room for fantasy. When he walked up the stairs, he could just barely hear the stairs creak amid the noise of the wind. He paused at the top of the stairs to pull the knife out of his overcoat pocket. He'd looked at the house carefully to remember what bedroom was Julie's, but now that he was *inside* the house, he wasn't completely sure. His hands were shaking from fear and cold. How could I possibly not know which room it is? Kurtz thought. Perhaps it was the lack of sleep or the mental exhaustion of the horrific trip from Leerton to Breda that confused him. Perhaps it was the fear that gripped his mind.

Four closed doors were in front of him, but he didn't quite know which one to choose. They weren't spaced in the perfect order he'd expected, and though he was almost certain which door was the right one, he wasn't completely sure. For a long moment, he felt like he was frozen in the spot where he was standing, even while he berated himself for not acting. He chose the first door to his right. He turned the flashlight off. He'd turn it back on again after he was completely inside the room. He put his hand on the cold door knob and turned it and went inside. He turned the flashlight back on but virtually the moment he did, the overhead light went on and he felt a tremendous blow on his head and collapsed to the ground.

When he woke up, the room was brightly lit, and the light hurt his eyes. It took him a moment to get used to it and see Jim Leiden and Bill Mathers sitting in front of him. It was about the same moment he realized his legs were shackled and his arms were handcuffed behind his back. Jim had called Mathers after he'd knocked Kurtz out, and Mathers had been able to make it to Julie's in one of the department's trucks. Jim had gotten stuck in the snow after he'd crossed into Michigan. He'd gotten a ride the rest of the way in a National Guard truck after he'd convinced the driver it was a life or death situation.

"You really fucked up this time, Kurtz," Mathers said.

"I—I don't know what you're talking about," Kurtz mumbled. "I got lost in the snow. I was afraid I was going to die if I didn't get inside somewhere."

"Why didn't you knock, then, instead of breaking in? And what were you doing with the knife and the gun and mace?" Jim said. "Were you going to shoot the snow if it didn't stop?"

"I started carrying weapons after the killings started. I didn't want to be murdered. Let me loose. I haven't done anything wrong. I don't even know whose house this is."

"There's no sense arguing about it, Kurtz," Mathers said. "You're dead meat. You'll never spend another night outside a jail cell. We already knew you were the Breda Killer. It was just a matter of proving it. We got enough evidence on you to fill up the *Encyclopedia Britannica*."

"This is an outrage. I demand to see an attorney."

"Sorry. I don't know any that make house calls. Especially in the middle of the worst snowstorm ever."

Julie came in. When Kurtz looked into her eyes, he realized instantly that she knew it was he who'd come to the door that day.

"So this little pipsqueak killed all those people?" Julie said. "Amazing, isn't it?"

"I haven't killed anyone! I'll sue the county, and I'll sue everyone here for everything you've got."

Mathers got up and looked out the window. The snow had finally stopped, and the first rosy tint of morning peeked over the white horizon.

"We might as well try to get him to the station," Mathers said to Jim. "It ain't gonna get any better for a long time, and I've got a lot of work to do. And I'm tired of socializing with this asshole. Kurtz, get up. I'm taking you to the county jail. Feel free to try to escape if you want. I'd love to have an excuse to kill you."

Chapter 14

To the few people who thought about it, it was surprising how fast—at least on the surface of things—Breda returned to normal. There was no celebration, but the haunted look, the fear that you could see on almost everyone's face before Kurtz was captured, disappeared almost immediately. Within a few days, as soon as the snow had been plowed and all the power lines had been restored, people would greet each other on the street as cheerfully as before the murders. Of course, the psychic wounds for most people would never heal completely, and for a few, the murders would haunt them for the rest of their lives, but most people at least made it seem as if they had put the murders behind them. It probably helped that Kurtz had taken his cyanide pill his first day in jail and killed himself. No one had to relive the agony of the murders during a trial or worry that somehow he would escape from jail. People started going out at night alone again, and just like before, folks would gather at Jim's store and stand around the wood stove and talk.

"Society's just gone bad all the way through," Jack Booth said there one day. "You never had murderers like Kurtz around when we still had law and order in this country."

Ham Marble wasn't so sure, but he thought for a moment and puffed on his pipe before he said anything.

"I don't know," he said. "This seemed to me like a special case. There's really nothing you can compare it to."

"If Wallace ever gets elected, we can get back to where we oughtta be," Jack said with a nod of his head for emphasis.

Jenelyn Robles had come in to buy bread and milk and overheard the men talking.

"Yeah, lynchings all over the South," she said. "Good old law and order."

"At least in the South they don't have nuts going around killing people like they do up here," Jack said.

"That's because there everybody's a nut, so nobody can tell the difference."

Julie came in.

"Guess what, Jim?" she said. "I've got some real interesting news: Bill Mathers and Jolene Van Riper are getting married. He's resigning as sheriff and they're moving to Florida."

Jim was surprised but didn't say anything while he digested the news. It didn't take Jack Booth long to digest it, though.

"Whatever happened to the one year waiting period?" he said. He was referring to the period of time it was once thought proper for widows to wait after their husband's death before seeing other men.

"That went out with hoop skirts and corsets," Jenelyn said.

"Reverend Van Riper is barely cold in his grave. No wonder they're slinking out of the state like rats."

"That sly dog," Jim said with a smile. "He never said anything about her to me, and we spent all that time together."

"I'm happy for them," Julie said. "I don't think it's scandalous. It's not like her husband died last week or something. It's so good to hear about something happy in this town again."

"Standards," Jack said. "That's what everybody's lost. Standards."

"Isn't Mathers at least going to arrest the rest of that Kurtz gang before he goes?" Keith Aacker said.

"The police don't think the others had anything to do with the murders," Jim said. "They thought Hinton was just as nutty as everybody else. He hardly had anything to do with the rest of the family. The whole thing turned out to be a lot simpler than anyone ever thought. Maybe that's why the case was so hard to solve. Everybody was looking for something really complicated."

Jim thought about the Death List that he'd painstakingly put together. No list of any kind had been found among Kurtz's belongings. He'd apparently just killed people in Breda at random, so it was almost a coincidence that all but one of them was on the list.

"How about that Kurtz that followed you home from Morrisey that time?"

"The police really don't think he was involved either. They figure he was just pissed off at me for trying to pin the murders on the Kurtz family and didn't have any idea his cousin was behind them. And besides, he denies it was him that followed me, and no one's ever been able to prove it."

"I still think they should have arrested the other Kurtzes," Booth said. "For good measure if nothing else."

"Speaking of marriages, when are you two gonna tie the knot?" Ham said to Jim and Julie.

"Well, since you asked, we're planning on getting married in May," Jim said.

Jim and Julie had decided that week but hadn't told anyone yet besides Julie's mother.

"Well, hey, that's great news," Keith said.

"Yes, it certainly is," Jenelyn said. "I'm so happy for you."

Even Booth seemed pleased to hear the news, and for the first time Jim felt like everything in Breda was back to normal again.

About the Author

Steven Arnett was born in Detroit, Michigan, and enjoys writing fiction and poetry. He has degrees from Michigan State University and the University of Maine. He currently lives in Johns Creek, Georgia, with his wife, Delphine, and daughter, Vivienne. His novels *Winners and Losers* and *Death on Lake Michigan* both received 5 star reviews from the Readers Favorite Web site.

A good place to start if you are interested in Steven Arnett's writings is his book of short stories. You can download a copy for free in several formats at https://goo.gl/Fa6RAS. That book provides a good illustration of the flavor and diversity of Mr. Arnett's work. It includes several stories that fall into the thriller/suspense genre, and many others as well. in available At https://goo.gl/ERSr1x you can get a Kindle copy of *The Short Stories of Steven Arnett* for $2.99 or a paperback version for $5.99.

All of Mr. Arnett's books can be purchased at his Amazon Author's Page at https://goo.gl/7CFnHE. The are available there in Kindle format and hard copy.

The Novels of Steven Arnett

Winners and Losers

Set in a small southern Michigan city in the early 1990s, the comedy novel *Winners and Losers* stars Tom Slotrak, a young man who wins the jackpot in the Michigan Lottery and the crazy and (sometimes) adventures he has afterwards. He learns the hard way that money can't buy happiness but that it sure can lead to some very funny and bizarre experiences!

A reviewer wrote this about *Winners and Losers*:

This book turned out to be one of the more enjoyable reads I've had in years. It's the first fiction book I can remember that kept me up reading too late at night and made me sorry it was over at the end. Skillfully written, lots of laugh-out-loud moments, unpredictable plot twists, and well-drawn characters. I've started a lot of fiction books in recent years and ended up quitting them, because I just wasn't enjoying them. This author hasn't forgotten that above all, a book should be fun to read.

Death on Lake Michigan

In the **5 star rated mystery novel** *Death on Lake Michigan*, Mike O'Brien, once the crusading editor of the *Michigan State News*, now the assistant editor of the *Gull Haven Observer*, becomes obsessed with solving the murder of Rich Mallon, one of the most notorious and well-known summer citizens of Gull Haven—and finds love in the process.

Reviewer Jack Magnus wrote this about *Death on Lake Michigan* for the Reader's Favorite Web site:

Steven Arnett's noir murder mystery, Death on Lake Michigan, is an adroit pairing of investigative sleuthing and police procedural as O'Brien and his buddy on the local police force, Detective George Dirkman of the Lake County Sheriff's Department, work in tandem in their attempt to solve the mystery. Arnett provides plenty of red herrings to give the reader his/her own opportunities to consider the clues and guess at the culprit. The Gull Haven location is inspired and lovely, and I wouldn't be at all surprised if other readers will be as tempted to visit that little beach town as much as I was. Arnett's Mike O'Brien is everything you'd want in a noir detective or, in this case, investigative sleuth. He's got an eye for women and is relatively fearless in his quest for the truth. Death on Lake Michigan is highly recommended.

The Labyrinth

At 3 o'clock in the morning cabin in Wells River, New Hampshire, a man who had called himself John Jones is run over by a car. He had been out walking in the rain miles away from where he lived, and there is no rational way to explain why. A strange drifter, he'd been living in a rundown cabin on Crawford's Hill for a few months, but no one had really got to know him. The local sheriff, Jeremy Wright, searches the cabin but can find only one thing that might help him identify John Jones or that would tell him anything about his life: A pile of manuscript. Could be a novel or could it be an autobiography? There was no easy way to tell, but he knew he'd have to take on the job of reading through it to looks for clues.

The Labyrinth, a romantic adventure wrapped in a thriller, chronicles John Jones's involvement in a murder when he was 15 years old that shaped his whole life afterward. It tells the story of how he ended up a thousand miles from where he had lived and grown up, in a place where he knew no one and no one knew him. His story ends up getting read by Jeremy, by his precocious 14 year old daughter, Mandy, his widowed mother, Dorothy, and George Teller, his English literature teacher brother-in-law. Each of them ends up with an entirely different picture of who John Jones was and even if that was really his name or if his story was true. They also end up with more questions than answers: Who really was John Jones? Does anyone really have a true identity, or does everyone really have a different identity to everyone who knows them or crosses their path in life?

A reviewer wrote this about *The Labyrinth*:

Labyrinth is really a gripping suspense thriller! A great, refreshing story, different from other thrillers. Readers are more interested in finding out the actual identity of John Jones than the motif of his assassination. It's a book impossible to put down that captivates from the very first page, and the story is wonderfully written. It's a must-read: absolutely riveting!

The Summer of Robert Byron

It's fall 1966, and Robert Byron has returned to his home town of Blue Spring in Michigan after serving in Vietnam. Everyone there tries to welcome him home, but he's unsocial and ends up alienating almost everyone. He pretty much keeps to himself through the winter, until the money he'd saved up in Vietnam runs outs, and he has to go back to work. He meets Jean Summers, a teacher at Blue Spring High School who'd just started her teaching career the previous fall herself, when Robert is hired by her landlord to do some work on the house she's renting. They're complete opposites in personality, but somehow, they're attracted to each other anyway. *The Summer of Robert Byron* is their story: Of how Jean tries to redeem through love Robert's alienation and the dark secret that he has brought home with him from the war. Can she succeed or is it too late to ever really bring him home again?

An Amazon reviewer posted this 5 star review about it: "Steven Arnett is my favorite new author. This doesn't disappoint. As another reviewer said, a romance, written by a man! Love."

Please like Steven Arnett's Author Page at
https://www.facebook.com/arnettse/info

You can search for postings about Steven Arnett's books
on Facebook using #stevenarnett